Live to Fly another Day

The Travel Mishaps of Caity Shaw
Book Five

Eliza Watson

Live to Fly Another Day

Books by Eliza Watson

Nonfiction

Genealogy Tips & Quips

Fiction

A Mags and Biddy Genealogy Mystery Series

How to Fake an Irish Wake (Book 1)
How to Snare a Dodgy Heir (Book 2)

The Travel Mishaps of Caity Shaw Series

Flying by the Seat of My Knickers (Book 1)
Up the Seine Without a Paddle (Book 2)
My Christmas Goose Is Almost Cooked (Book 3)
My Wanderlust Bites the Dust (Book 4)
Live to Fly Another Day (Book 5)
When in Doubt Don't Chicken Out (Book 6)

Women's Fiction Books

Kissing My Old Life Au Revoir

Romance

Under Her Spell
Identity Crisis
'Til Death Do Us Part

Writing Young Adult as Beth Watson

Getting a Life, Even if You're Dead

To my sister, and fellow author, Penny Wolberg
for inspiring my love of writing.

ACKNOWLEDGMENTS

Thank you to my husband, Mark, for taking the ferry with me from Ireland to England to research this book. And a big thank you for driving while we were there. To Charlotte, Des, Mags, and Darragh for helping me polish Declan's dialogue. Our Irish slang sessions are always great craic. To all my friends and family for believing in me and supporting my writing in so many ways. I would have given up years ago without your encouragement. To Nikki Ford, Elizabeth Wright, and Meghan Lloyd for your in-depth feedback, helping to make this a stronger book. To Sandra and Judy Watson for reading the book several times.

To Dori Harrell for your fab editorial skills. To Chrissy Wolfe for your final proofreading tweaks. Thanks to you ladies I can always publish a book with confidence. To Lyndsey Lewellen for another incredible cover and for capturing the spirit of Caity. And to Amy Atwell at Author E.M.S. for a flawless interior format and for always promptly answering my many questions.

Thanks to my brilliant fans who began this adventure with Caity in *Flying by the Seat of My Knickers* and who continue to follow her journey. A special shout-out to Caity fan Nicole Duvall, who won my contest to have a character named after her!

My Coffey Family Tree
Cheat Sheet

Great-grandparents
Patrick Coffey & Mary Flannery

Michael   Ellen Quinn   Theresa Lynch   Agnes   Grandma Bridget

           Seamus   Catherine Ryan   m. John Michael Daly   m. Frederico Brunetti

                        Sadie Collentine   George Wood   Teri

                        Julia Smyth   Dottie

                                                                     Mom

                                                                              Rachel

                                                                              Me

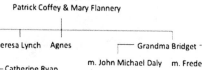
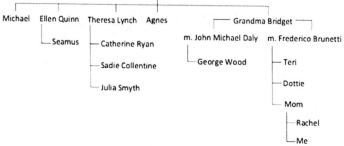

CHAPTER ONE

Little Caity on the Bog. Laura Ingalls, I was not. I'd never have survived traveling out west in a covered wagon and settling on a Minnesota prairie. And I might not survive glamping on Ireland's west coast. Rather than enjoying a pint of Guinness at my first St. Patrick's Day parade in Dublin, I was drinking tea, shivering inside the gypsy caravan that reeked like cow dung and my parents' musty basement. The wind howled and rain pelted against the soft-top roof.

Gemma, my coworker at Flanagan's beer, had weaseled her way into working the holiday event, so I was now stuck conducting a site inspection for a rustic team-building retreat. It would have been my first time managing a group, proving I could handle my new position. Instead, Gemma was once again on-site for an event my sister, Rachel, had planned, proving she *couldn't* manage it.

A loud moo sounded outside the caravan.

I jumped up from the lower bunk bed, hitting my head on the top one. Zoe hopped off the purple beanbag chair. The brightly colored bohemian furnishings did little to perk up my mood.

"We have a visitor," Zoe said.

My friend—and my boyfriend Declan's sister—had agreed to join me on my glamping adventure when she'd seen the website with rolling green hills and quaint stone fences, the blue Atlantic Ocean on the horizon. It hadn't mentioned that we'd be *in* a field with cows and that the scenic ocean could only be viewed from the end of the long dirt road leading to the site in County Galway.

Zoe opened the wooden door, and a gust of wind about blew it off the hinges. I brushed my hair from my eyes to find an escaped cow staring up at us with big brown eyes, its front hooves on the bottom step.

"Can cows climb stairs?" I said.

"I would think, but it's much too big to fit between the handrails. Isn't it?"

I shrugged.

The cow placed a hoof on the second step, apparently taking offense with Zoe's *too big* comment. Zoe and I leaned back.

"You did a bril job herding Carrig's sheep off the road and back into the field at Christmas. Want to give this a go?"

I shook my head, staring down the cow. "What if it charges me?"

"If it's gonna charge anything, it'd be this bright-red caravan. But it's not a bull." A look of inspiration filled Zoe's blue eyes. "What a fab team-building event. See which team can herd cows back into the field first. Or at all."

"Sounds like a liability issue."

"Have them sign waivers. What a gas. A bunch of suits herding cows. That would go viral and make you a few quid."

"It'd get me fired. Maybe we could do cow-dung bingo. Although, not sure how that could be a team-building event."

Zoe's forehead crinkled in confusion.

"It's a fundraiser," I said. "A fenced-in area is marked off with numbered squares, and each one is sold for, like, five bucks. A cow is turned loose and determines the winner by making the first cow pie in one of the squares."

The cow let out a moo and clomped a hoof down on the step.

"Don't think it likes the idea," Zoe said.

I had to come up with some killer team-building events to impress my boss. There'd been friction among the executives, and the CEO insisted they learn to work together by roughing it. He'd canceled the five-star Scottish castle hotel where I could be relaxing in the spa right now, enjoying a mani and pedi, sipping a mimosa.

The cow placed its other front hoof on the second step.

"Its shoulders fit, but it'll get stuck at the belly," Zoe said.

As if to prove Zoe wrong, the animal proceeded up another step, its back hooves now on the bottom one, its middle squeezed between the handrails. It let out a distressed moo, wriggling around. Its head swiveled from side to side.

Zoe and I jumped back.

"Bloody hell! It's stuck. What are we gonna do with a stuck cow?"

Mr. Donovan, the grounds' owner, an elderly man dressed in red wellies and a worn tan jacket, ambled up, shaking his head at the cow. "Sorry 'bout that, luvs. Don't know how this one keeps getting loose." He swept a calming hand over the cow's back. "You're all right there, not stuck, ya aren't. Just a bit frightened is all." He guided the cow down the few steps to freedom.

Zoe and I let out relieved sighs.

The man eyed our matching green tutus with gold sparkly shamrocks over our jeans. "Heading down to the pub to celebrate, are ya?"

Zoe had made the tutus when we thought we'd be participating in Dublin's holiday festivities. We were bundled up in green wool sweaters, scarves, and gloves. I had on my purple wellies, a Christmas present from Zoe and Declan's family. The tourists hadn't yet arrived for the season, so our outfits were a bit more festive than the locals'. The glamp grounds didn't open until April 1 but had accommodated us because the owner was my boss's uncle.

"No, we're going kayaking." A gust of wind blew Zoe's scarf and long blond hair against her face. "At least checking out the cove where they can do it. Which reminds me. The sink in the main building is banjaxed. Water doesn't seem to be working."

The man nodded. "Aye, was coming to tell ya a water pipe broke in town."

"When will it be fixed?" I asked.

"Not today I suppose, seeing as the lads are in the pub celebrating. Don't think ya want them to be fixing a pipe."

"So we won't have water until tomorrow?" I said.

He shrugged, rubbing his chin. "Possibly the next, I'd say. They might be recovering from a few too many jars. Things can be a bit lacksy-daisy o'er the holiday."

Suddenly, the grounds' community showers didn't sound so bad. No way was I going two days without a shower or water.

"And don't be flushing a toilet more than once," he said.

Seriously? The women's restroom only had two toilets. There'd better be more than that in the men's room, or I'd be using a urinal for the first, and hopefully only, time in my life. No way was a bladder infection going to be my souvenir from this trip.

"'Tis a government conspiracy, the broken pipe." His face reddened. "People weren't paying the new water bills, so they had to refund the money to those who did. Ended up taking a loss on the whole bloody mess. So now the water company is getting revenge on us all." He walked off with the cow, grumbling about water bills, property taxes, the price of petrol...

"How did people just not pay their water bills?" I said.

"My mum and dad didn't pay it. People were livid."

If I could refuse to pay bills, I wouldn't be such a financial wreck. Maybe that would be an added bonus of living in Ireland. However, I had to obtain Irish citizenship to live here, which was proving more difficult than I'd anticipated.

Fifteen minutes later, we were almost to the end of the muddy road when Zoe's small blue car got stuck in a rut. She floored it, which did nothing but cause an awful noise and smell.

She smacked a palm against the steering wheel. "Bloody hell!" Her gaze darted to me. "Gonna have to give us a push."

"A push?"

"Don't think it will take much. Seems close to moving."

I pulled my jacket hood up over my head and stepped out into the rain. I placed my hands firmly against the back of the car and pushed with all my strength while Zoe pressed on the accelerator. Nothing. I gave it another push. The car flew forward, and I fell down. My hands braced my fall, preventing my face from hitting the ground, but muddy water splashed all over me. I raised myself up on all fours.

Zoe hopped out of the car. "Are you all right?" When she saw me, she burst out laughing.

"It isn't funny," I whined. "There's no water to shower."

"It's great craic."

I started laughing so I didn't cry.

Zoe held out a hand and helped me up. I was tempted to pull her down in the mud with me after she'd laughed, but I didn't have the energy. I shrugged off my muddy raincoat and tutu and threw them in the trunk. My other pair of jeans was still wet from getting caught in the rain yesterday while traipsing through a deserted village, planning a scavenger hunt.

Zoe placed a plastic bag on the seat for me to sit on.

She grabbed a pair of green-and-blue plaid flannel pants and a green sweatshirt from the backseat. She sniffed the clothes and handed them to me. "They're clean. I always keep an extra outfit in my car in case of an emergency."

I peeled off my wet jeans and slipped on the flannel bottoms. At least the outfit was green since my tutu was trashed.

"Look how well we worked together as a team," she said. "Another bril idea. The first team to get a car out of the muddy drive wins. Or maybe you could use dune buggies rather than cars..."

"How about whatever team best survives glamping wins?"

It wouldn't be me.

Escape rooms were all the rage right now for team-building events. Attendees would definitely be motivated to escape their caravans and the glamping site.

Zoe pulled onto the main road and flipped the windshield wipers into panic mode. We encountered a flooded corner, and water splashed against the windows. "Sure hope they don't close the bridge from Achill Island to the mainland."

"Would they do that?"

"No clue. Maybe if there are gale-force winds and flooding."

"I'm not staying in that caravan in gale-force winds."

"Maybe we should stop for a pint until the rain lets up."

"I think we could drink a *keg* and it'll still be raining."

"Have to make sure we use the loo before we leave the pub, to conserve on toilet flushes."

My phone rang. I finally had service. I scrambled to grab it from my purse, hoping it was Declan. Rather than Declan's twinkling blue eyes and charming smile, I was greeted by Gemma's green-shadowed eyes and *Irish Princess* tiara crowning the top of her stylish blond do. I smoothed a hand over my wet and windblown auburn hair and wiped a blotch of mud from my face with a dirty hand.

"The restaurant your sister supposedly booked doesn't have space for the group. It was never confirmed."

"Of course, it was confirmed." Rachel didn't screw up. Why hadn't Gemma called to reconfirm yesterday?

"She's not answering her phone."

"Because it's four a.m. in Milwaukee."

"So what should we do about her messing up?"

What was with this "we" thing? She was in Dublin while I was in the boonies. Yet I didn't want it to come back on Rachel, even though it was surely Gemma's fault. She'd probably taken them to the wrong place or was lying to sabotage Rachel's job with Brecker, a US-based beer corporation that owned Flanagan's Irish beer. She thought Rachel and I had conspired to steal her job, even though she was an admin assistant, not a meeting planner. Rachel had been against me approaching Flanagan's CEO about creating an internal planner position, insisting I was too inexperienced. My sister had been right.

"I'll call you right back," I said.

I disconnected and growled at the phone. Gemma was my new Gretchen. However, my former coworker Gretchen and I were on better terms, which was why I hadn't yet told her I was coming up empty on her ancestry research. Wish I could say the same about my client Nigel's family tree, which I'd stumbled across online. I was dreading telling him that his family didn't come from blue blood. Far from it.

I called Gerry Coffey. The owner of Coffey's pub in Dublin was Rachel's love interest and my landlord, renting me a studio apartment above the pub.

"A happy Paddy's Day to ya, Caity Shaw," Gerry said.

I tried to sound as cheery as he did and recounted the group's situation in a nutshell. If anyone was motivated to get Rachel out of a bind, it was Gerry.

"No worries, luv. I'll block off an area of the bar for them. Can teach 'em how to pull a pint."

"Awesome. Do you have any Coffey T-shirts you can put on the bill?"

"Just received an entire lot of them. My sister is here. She can teach them a bit of step dancing."

"Thanks a mil. I owe you one."

"Well, seeing as you're offering, ya know what I'd be liking?"

"Rachel?"

"Absolutely brilliant, ya are."

According to Rachel, he'd already *had* her in every room of his townhouse at Christmastime, the last time they'd seen each other. Yet Rachel claimed they were only friends.

"Three more days and she'll be here."

We were going to visit our newfound rellies in the Midlands and then off to England to see George, my mom's half brother. I'd met George for the first time last month when he'd tracked me down while I was working in Prague.

I thanked Gerry and was preparing to call Gemma back when a text came through from Mom.

No luck.

My stomach dropped.

She still hadn't found Grandma's birth certificate.

I needed her birth, marriage, and death records to apply for Irish citizenship. If I could even locate her baptismal certificate, I could submit it with a notarized letter from the Irish registrar's office stating a birth certificate wasn't on file. The only proof I had of her living in Ireland was her engagement picture taken at a Dublin photography studio prior to marrying her first husband in *England*. A large envelope containing my citizenship application and the other required documents was waiting to be mailed once I found Grandma's birth record.

One of my selling points to my Irish boss was that I was eligible for dual citizenship, making the job transfer from a temporary Brecker contractor to full-time Flanagan employee seamless. Not being a Brecker employee, I wasn't eligible for an intracompany transfer. Even if I was, there were a slew of restrictions. If I told my boss I was unable to get citizenship, it might be grounds for termination. It would also demonstrate my lack of planning skills.

Obtaining Irish citizenship, so I wasn't deported when my ninety-day allowable stay expired, was becoming a bigger threat to losing my new job than nasty Gemma.

CHAPTER TWO

I'd barely slept, thanks to Zoe's snoring, rain pelting against the soft-topped caravan, and knowing Gemma was toasty warm in her hotel bed. The following day, it was still pouring at noon, so Zoe and I left before the roads were closed due to flooding.

And all the toilets had been flushed. Having to resort to using a urinal would have been my breaking point. We'd parked the car at the end of the muddy drive to ensure our getaway. Luckily, I only had to schlepp a small carry-on bag a mile to the vehicle. We'd been driving for a few minutes when a delayed text came through from Declan. A pic of him dressed in a green-and-black plaid kilt, black shirt, and black knee-high socks.

Be still my heart.

There was something insanely sexy about a guy who was confident enough to wear a kilt. I rarely wore a skirt without tights, thanks to an ugly scar on my knee from when I was eight and had fallen on my bike wheel's spokes. I'd been a major klutz from an early age.

I FaceTimed Declan despite no makeup and not having washed my hair for five days. He answered, dressed in a white polo shirt and tan slacks. Very disappointing.

"Your text just came through. Put the kilt back on."

A sly smile curled his lips. "Right, then, that's a change. Usually you're asking me to be taking clothes off."

I went warm all over, smiling.

"Ack!" Zoe hollered. "I'm not listening to my brother have FaceTime sex."

"Oh yeah, your sister's here." I directed the phone at Zoe, who gave him a wave. We hadn't seen each other in two weeks, and I'd be all over FaceTime sex if Zoe wasn't there. "The glamping trip was a bust. It poured the entire time, yet we had no running water. Go figure."

"Not to gloat, but it's twenty-four here, about seventy-five Fahrenheit." A breeze playfully tousled his short, wavy brown hair. "Taking the entire lot of 'em on a catamaran cruise."

Declan was in Malta, located in the Mediterranean somewhere between Sicily and Africa. I'd looked it up. He'd be home in two days to go to the Midlands with Rachel and me. Malta would be his last trip abroad. He'd canceled six months of back-to-back meeting jobs to work local events and spend time with me.

Fingers crossed I'd *be* there to spend time with.

The sparkle in Declan's blue eyes dimmed. "My house sold."

"Woot!" Zoe punched a celebratory fist in the air.

Yet Declan didn't look nearly as excited.

I smiled. "That's great. Isn't it?"

"Yeah, of course, it's grand. Just surprised it sold so fast."

Declan had lived in the house with his wife, Shauna, before she'd passed away three years ago. He'd been renting it out since her death. It held a lot of memories.

"Any luck on your granny's birth certificate?" he asked, changing the subject.

I shook my head. "Mom and my aunts have searched everywhere. Either my grandma managed to obtain US naturalization without one, or she destroyed it, trying to hide her past. My aunt Teri remembers my grandpa saying he'd obtained his driver's license by sending a quarter into the DMV. I don't think they were nearly as strict about documentation back then."

"Forget the birth certificate," Zoe said. "You two get married and you'll be a citizen. And now that Declan sold his house, you can buy a place to live."

A look of panic seized Declan's face. My heart hammered. We didn't even plan on being roomies. We certainly weren't buying a house together. Zoe and I hoped to share an apartment if she found a job in Dublin after she graduated from college in May. I'd been too quick to shack up with my ex-boyfriend Andy, and moving out had been a complete nightmare. Not that Declan was anything like that narcissistic controlling bastard, or that we'd ever break up. But I finally had my first apartment without a man's help, proving I could stand on my own.

"Why are you two acting so weird?" Zoe said, breaking the silence.

"We're not," we both said.

I shot her a warning glance.

"Right, then," Declan said. "Keep me posted on the certificate. I'm sure you'll find it."

Declan and I avoided the topic of what would happen if I didn't locate it.

"Yep. Keep me posted on the apartment hunting." I wanted him to know I hadn't taken Zoe's comment seriously. And that her crazy idea about us getting married hadn't been *mine*.

We said our awkward good-byes and hung up.

Zoe laughed. "Well, if he wasn't motivated to find your granny's birth certificate before, he is now."

"That wasn't funny."

"Bloody well was."

"What if he thinks I've been talking to you about us getting married?"

"You two will get married. Why not do it a wee bit sooner than planned?"

Some people married for love, some for money. I loved Declan, but I didn't want him to think I was marrying him for my Irish citizenship. Honestly, he wouldn't think that, but I didn't want our family and friends to question our decision if and when we did get married. My moving here might have been on a bit of a whim, but you didn't marry on a whim in Ireland when it took five years to get a divorce.

We stopped by Coffey's pub to tell Gerry we'd returned early so he didn't have to walk Mac, the Irish terrier that I'd won at Christmas. Bernice and Gracie— two event attendees turned genealogy clients—had entered me in the contest while I'd been escorting a Dublin consumer promotion. Besides not having had the time to research bringing a dog into the US and the financial responsibility, I'd lived with my parents. Mom would not have appreciated dog sitting while I was jet-setting around the world. Growing up, I'd had a cat and a hamster. Mac seemed to sense that he was my first dog and was taking full advantage of my inferior dog-training skills.

The day after St. Patrick's Day, the pub was still decked out for the holiday. Up-lighting washed the long wooden bar in green, and a lively traditional Irish tune competed with the chatter. Shamrock streamers ran the length of the walls, which displayed soccer, rugby, and hurling team memorabilia.

Zoe pushed her way through the crush of people toward the bathroom.

A woman in a low-cut strapless green dress with a black belt, green velvet top hat, and black thigh-high pantyhose was flirting shamelessly with Gerry. The pub owner was fortyish with short dark hair, blue eyes, and biceps big enough to stop an occasional brawl. He had on a green *Coffey's Dublin* T-shirt.

As if feeling my curious stare, he glanced over at me with an uneasy smile. "Jaysus, what happened to ya?"

I thought I looked pretty good for having taken a sponge bath with rainwater and slept in my outfit— Zoe's flannel pants and sweatshirt—too cold to change into my jammies. I recounted our adventure.

He poured a Flanagan's cider ale over ice and placed the glass on the bar. "Sounds like you could be using a jar."

"Maybe two."

I took a sip, savoring the sweet apple taste. A Guinness would hit the spot, but it'd be just my luck Gemma would wander in and catch me drinking a competitor's brand. I'd rather get fired for not having dual citizenship than to give Gemma the satisfaction of getting me canned. Five months ago on my first trip to Ireland, I'd taken a pic of my first Guinness. I'd never imagined that I would one day be referring to it as a *local* brew and to Flanagan's as my *employer's* ale.

"How did everything go with the group?" I asked.

"Grand. That Gemma is a bit daft though, isn't she? Sat here telling me how Rachel had screwed up the entire event even though I told her I knew Rachel quite well."

"Yeah, she's a trip." Speaking of knowing Rachel quite well, I peered over at the slutty leprechaun giving me the evil eye.

"Just a friend," Gerry said.

I raised a skeptical brow.

"All right." He lowered his voice. "Maybe a wee bit more than a friend. We date on occasion. It's not like Rachel doesn't see other blokes."

"She doesn't."

A pleased smile curled his lips. "Doesn't she now?"

Rachel was going to kill me. She'd have lied and said she dated on a weekly basis. She didn't have time to date. She'd liked the idea of me living above Gerry so he could babysit me, but she'd made me promise not to discuss their relationship. Did that include not telling her about the slutty leprechaun?

I shrugged. "I really shouldn't say. I haven't seen her lately to know if she dates or not."

I didn't blame Gerry for dating other people. He and Rachel only saw each other every few months, and she sent him mixed signals. But when I stopped by for a pint after work, the conversation always turned to Rachel. He was totally gaga over her.

"You need to discuss this with Rachel. It's not my place to tell her about *that*." I slid a sideways glance toward the chick still staring at us.

Gerry nodded faintly. "Have you heard anything on your citizenship?"

I shook my head. "They say it can take up to six months."

Or *never* if I didn't find Grandma's birth certificate.

I hadn't told Gerry about my challenges because I hadn't told Rachel. She'd blow a gasket that I'd gone for the job *on a whim* and without her blessing before confirming my ability to obtain citizenship. Plan B was to get a work permit, which was no easy task. The employer had to have advertised, attempting to hire an Irish citizen. And over a hundred occupations were ineligible for job permits, including a slew of administrative and clerical jobs, under which my position was categorized. The list of regulations was overwhelming.

I really needed to work on a plan C.

Gerry snagged a business card by the cash register on the back bar. "Scottish couple was in here last night, searching for their Coffey rellies, wondering if we might be related." He handed me the card. "Told them mine hailed from County Cork. They believe theirs were from County Westmeath."

Gerry and I'd met on my first Dublin meeting with Rachel. She'd located the Coffey surname pub hoping we might be related through Grandma's Coffey family. If we were, it was likely four generations twice removed.

"Even if you're not related to them, they're interested in hiring your services." He headed down the bar to refill a few pints.

If the couple turned out to be related, I'd give them a family discount. I was too poor to be overly generous. However, I wasn't feeling particularly qualified to be charging people at all. And I really didn't need one more family tree to *not* be able to trace. Besides Grandma's birth record, I hadn't found McKinney rellies for Bernice and Gracie to visit on their Scotland trip this summer. I'd found zip on Gretchen's German grandpa. And it had been sheer luck I'd discovered Nigel's ancestor's horrific past while perusing family trees online.

Nigel's grandfather believed he was the result of his mother's affair with a married blue-blooded aristocrat. Actually, his father had remained unidentified because he'd been a felon, shipped off to Australia to serve a life sentence. At least he'd been convicted of burglary and not murder. Yet there was nothing worse than debunking stories passed down through generations, deeply ingrained in a family's identity. Like Gretchen planning to retire in a quaint Bavarian mountain village because the grandpa she'd never known had been German. What if I finally found his records and he turned out to be Danish? I once read Denmark didn't even have mountains. What if I discovered Bernice and Gracie's ancestor was *German* when they'd paid for a trip to *Scotland*?

I slipped the business card into my pocket. "You probably have tourists in here quite a bit looking for Coffey ancestors."

Gerry nodded. "Maybe you should give me a stack of business cards to hand out."

Maybe I should make some business cards.

"Could give a stash to my mates Jimmy Reilly and William Cavanaugh. They surely have tourists in their pubs all the time looking for relations."

Would the Irish government issue me a work permit if I worked for *myself*?

Five months ago I'd been completely adrift, no sense of who I was or what I wanted to be. Researching Grandma's ancestry and discovering my Irish roots had given me a sense of identity, direction, purpose, importance, pride...a sense of everything!

I pitied the poor immigration officer who had to drag my butt on a plane back to the States.

❧ ❧

Three types of people lived above a pub. Those who wanted to drink until all hours and not have to drive home with the stricter drunk-driving laws. Ones like me who needed cheap rent rather than a view of Saint Stephen's Green. And the elderly who couldn't hear the noise below. When my neighbor Fiona's TV wasn't blaring, she was hosting her ukulele group. A lively Irish tune came from her apartment, and Zoe and I did a little jig while I unlocked the door.

We entered the studio apartment, and Mac jumped up from my deflated bed and raced over to greet us.

I pointed at the flattened sheet of plastic. "Didn't Mommy tell you to stay off that so your claws didn't put a hole in it?" I let out a frustrated groan. "I had it leaning against the wall. He must have knocked it over."

His tail wagged despite his green tutu, which matched Zoe's and mine. He stared up at me with happy brown eyes, his tail going faster. Caving, I swept a hand over his tan fur and spoke in that cutesy pet-owner voice that used to annoy me. "Did you miss Mama? I can't blame you for acting up when Mommy was gone, can I? But you have three beds, and now Mommy has none."

"Watch it. Your scolding might make him cry. He sucks you right in, playing on your guilt."

"I know, but he's so stinking cute."

"And naughty."

I pulled off my purple wellies and placed them on the mat by the door. I tossed my coat over the back of a red couch Declan's parents had given me. Gerry had donated a wooden chair and small desk, which was my work area and dining table. Flanagan's allowed me to work from home two days a week. However, when I wasn't at the office, I worried about what Gemma was doing to sabotage my job. Out of sight, out of mind. And as a new employee, I needed to get to know my coworkers.

LIVE TO FLY ANOTHER DAY   21

"What the bloody hell is that?" Zoe pointed under the table at a pile of colorful yarn that looked like a rat's nest.

Mac had chewed Zoe's knitted hats to bits. She'd been knitting pet apparel like a maniac, preparing for a craft show with her grandma and aunt that weekend. Their family's cottage industry helped her pay for college and stash away money for the decorating shop she planned to open. I'd be her first client. My only wall décor was Declan's sketch of me and the framed watercolors of the Charles Bridge in Prague.

Zoe marched over and snatched the mutilated cardboard box off the floor. She shook the box, glaring at Mac. "This was on the table, where you aren't supposed to be. Naughty. Very naughty."

Mac whimpered and hid behind me.

"I'm not protecting you. Zoe's right. That was very bad. Why can't you be more like Esmé?"

Esmé was the cocker spaniel at Madame Laurent's hotel in Paris. The well-trained dog had escorted me to my guest room upon check-in, greeted me nightly on my return to the hotel, and welcomed me each morning at breakfast. The only time she'd disobeyed me was when she insisted on sleeping with me. She turned out to be better than sleeping meds.

"Now your mommy is going to have to learn to knit and help Auntie Zoe replace all the hats you wrecked."

"I can't knit."

"Then teach your son to."

"But I'll replace the yarn." I took a twenty euro bill from my purse and gave it to Zoe.

"Thanks. I'll go buy more yarn." She grabbed Mac's

leash off a hook by the door. "And you need to walk off some of that energy." She opened the door. It took some coaxing, and a few treats, for Mac to go along willingly.

Sending Mac to obedience school would be much cheaper than replacing everything he destroyed.

I flipped on the water kettle next to the microwave on top of a small dorm-size fridge in the kitchenette. I selected a purple floral teacup from my growing collection on a shelf. Besides a half dozen cups from Grandma's collection, our Irish rellie Sadie Collentine had given me a shamrock-and-ivy patterned one from our Flannery family's china factory in County Wicklow. A family I had yet to research. My cups also included a red floral one from Emily Ryan—the sister of Grandma's first husband, Michael Daly—and a gold-and-yellow patterned one from my genealogy client Nigel, a hotel banquet captain in Prague.

The place was sparsely decorated, but it was mine.

I wasn't required to have my ex's approval before hanging something on the wall, and I didn't have to make the bed daily. I didn't even *own* a bed. That would send Andy over the edge.

I smiled at the sense of freedom.

I'd brought the bare necessities from home knowing I'd possibly be returning there after ninety days until I straightened out my citizenship. I could not lose my job. My deferred student loan kicked in this month, and taxes were due in twenty-eight days. I should have listened to Mom and set aside money each paycheck for taxes. However, paying off store credit cards had been good for my self-esteem. Despite feeling inept at genealogy research, I needed the extra income. Yet I couldn't contact that Scottish couple until I'd completed the research for my existing clients, who'd paid in advance. Before long Gretchen would be pounding on my door, demanding answers. She had enough frequent flyer miles to show up at my apartment on a weekly basis.

I made a cup of Barry's Gold tea and took a calming sip as I sat at my desk to return an e-mail to George, my half uncle. Next week I'd finally visit the Daly Estate in England, where Grandma had lived with her first husband, Michael, and son, George. After her husband's death, she'd left her one-year-old son with Michael's cousin. Still coming to terms with having a half brother, Mom had decided to wait and come over with her sisters Teri and Dottie this summer so they could meet as a family.

An e-mail sat in my inbox from Sadie Collentine. Her son had recently set her up an e-mail account so we didn't have to rely on snail mail. I'd asked her and her cousin Seamus to verify their mothers' birth locations. Knowing where Grandma's sisters were born could help me pinpoint Grandma's birthplace.

Sadie's e-mail confirmed Seamus's mother, Ellen, and her mother, Theresa, had been born in Killybog, County Westmeath. The birth certificates were on file with the registrar's office in Mullingar. Ellen's mother's name had been left blank. No wonder I'd been unable to locate it in the civil records online index. Sadie recalled that Theresa's parents hadn't agreed on a name at her time of birth. Theresa later wrote in her first name, and it was never questioned.

What if Grandma's first name wasn't listed on her birth certificate? Would the Irish government accept that as a legal document for my citizenship?

I e-mailed Nicholas Turney an update on these family birth certificates. The local historian, who lived near Declan's parents, had helped me sort out my Coffey family tree. He was one of many I'd recruited for assistance in my quest for Grandma's birth record. Hopefully, he could go to the registrar's office and search for variables like a missing first name and alternate birth years. Grandma having lied about her age would have been minor compared to all the other secrets she'd kept.

CHAPTER
THREE

The next morning, I was running early and didn't have to holler down the street for the bus driver to wait as he closed the door. I claimed the only open seat and booted up my laptop. I spent my daily work commute doing genealogy research. I perused Scotland's vital records website, hoping Bernice and Gracie's ancestor's baptismal record had miraculously appeared since the last dozen times I'd checked.

According to Nicholas Turney, the Scottish had adhered to a family naming pattern, same as the Irish. Based on the 1871 Canadian census for James McKinney's family, his firstborn son, John, would have been named after James's father and the second-born daughter after his mother. That would mean his parents were John and Mary. However, out of the five James McKinneys born in Glasgow during that era, none were born to a John and Mary. I once again tried murdering the surname's spelling and using various birth years for James, but I still came up empty.

I heaved a frustrated sigh, glancing out the window. My gaze darted around at the unfamiliar surroundings.

Where the hell was I?

I'd taken the wrong bus!

The bus pulled up to a stop. I flew from my seat. Laptop tucked under my arm, I excused myself, pushing past people standing in the aisles. I hopped off. No clue where I was at, I ordered an Uber. The car arrived in six minutes, but it took us thirty-three minutes with traffic to get across town to Flanagan's headquarters.

I raced inside the glass building, scanned my company badge, and smiled calmly at the security guard. While riding the elevator up, I took a deep breath and tried not to look frazzled. I exited on the top floor and speed walked toward my desk, smiling as I passed coworkers in the hallway. I said good morning to Ita—a cheerful younger woman two cubicles down from me—arriving at my desk with a minute to spare. I dropped my laptop bag on the desk next to a photo of Declan dressed in a blue pilot's uniform, me in a powder-blue flight attendant one, the Eiffel Tower in the background. Halloween in Paris. I was waiting for the day I came in to find the picture of me in the sausage costume on my desk. Gemma obviously hadn't figured out it was me in the pic with the CEO hanging on her office wall.

I stared at the insanely hot photo of Declan while smoothing a hand over my flat-ironed hair. I swiped a pale-red gloss across my lips before booting up my laptop to compile my glamping site inspection notes. If my boss inquired about my citizenship status at our 9:00 a.m. meeting, I'd have to be vague. Something I'd become quite skilled at during my stint as an on-site meeting contractor. Attendees were always asking me questions I didn't have answers to.

An hour later, I walked into the CEO's outer office, where Gemma sat in a black leather chair behind a black steel-framed desk. The black furnishings were about as welcoming as her blue-eyed glare. My royal-blue designer dress and black heels helped me exude false confidence. She had no clue I was still paying on the pricey wardrobe I'd purchased to live up to Andy's expensive tastes and unrealistic expectations.

"How was the glamping trip?" Gemma smirked, twirling a clump of blond hair around her finger. She'd had her green sparkly nails done for the St. Patrick's Day celebration.

Wench.

"Awesome. It's going to give me the chance to plan some really creative events. Something unique they've never done before." I made it sound like this would be my shining hour.

Her smile faded.

Thankfully, the CEO was available, so I didn't have to have a glaring contest with Gemma that might end in a brawl that even Gerry Coffey wouldn't be able to break up.

I sat in the black leather chair in front of Matthew McHugh's desk. He was fiftyish, tall, with salt-and-pepper hair. He had on a brown cashmere suit jacket, blue oxford shirt, and dark jeans.

"How was it?" He gave me a kind smile.

The type of smile that almost made me want to fess up and admit my delayed citizenship status.

"Never done anything quite like it. A very unique experience."

"Just what I'm looking for. Something different. How are the cottages?"

"You've never been there?"

He shook his head. "Paddy just bought the place two years ago. A retirement venture."

Great. Now I felt obligated to be up front so it didn't come back to bite me in the butt. Yet I couldn't let his rellie's place sound as horrible as it'd been.

"The caravans are very colorful, and it's a quiet area except for an occasional moo. One cow got out a few times and paid us a visit."

He laughed. "Sounds perfect."

"A water pipe broke in town, so we were without water for a few days. Yet it rained a lot."

"Good thing it broke now. What's the chance of that happening twice in two months?"

Above average, with my luck.

I presented my ideas for a scavenger hunt at the island's deserted village with over eighty abandoned dwellings. A rock-climbing adventure that would give teams the satisfaction of helping each other scale a low-lying cliff. And Zoe's idea of herding cows back in the field. He seemed to like the whole cow slant.

"Rustic. Just what we need. Like one of those survivalist TV shows. Thanks for checking it out. I knew you were the right person for it. Gemma isn't really the roughing-it kind."

Talk about a backhanded compliment. I was made of sturdier stock than fragile-flower Gemma, so now I'd get all the shit jobs?

Gemma knocked, then entered with a contract to be signed.

While scanning the document, the CEO said, "Oh, and great job finding a new venue last minute for the St. Patrick's Day group."

"My pleasure," Gemma and I said simultaneously.

I glared at her, and she smiled innocently, avoiding my gaze. I couldn't believe she'd thrown Rachel under the bus and then took credit for finding a new venue. Bitch.

Our boss gave us a curious stare. "Ah, okay." He blew off the awkward situation and handed Gemma the signed contract.

She sashayed out without looking at me.

Rachel would go ballistic.

"The August incentive this year is between Vienna, Florence, and Dubrovnik. You should start looking into costs to see which will work best as far as budget."

Prague would work best since I'd never even heard of *Dubrovnik*. Or how about Dublin's Connelly Court Hotel, where I'd stayed three times? A preferred vendor, their contracts were likely cut and dried. I'd never negotiated a hotel contract, done banquet guarantees, or anything planning related except check hotel and restaurant availability for Rachel's meetings. I couldn't turn to my sister for help. She'd warned me I'd be in over my head. My heart hammered.

"If you could compile a cost comparison by the end of next week, that'd be grand."

I'd have to cram my first twenty-hour online meeting planning course into this weekend. Maybe it was a good thing the program wouldn't be held in

Ireland, as I might not be allowed back in the country for ninety days if I was forced to leave in June.

Wait a sec. Did that mean I wouldn't be allowed in *any* EU country?

I took a calming breath before I hyperventilated and fainted on the CEO's desk. I refused to admit to my boss, or myself, that a glamping trip was more my speed.

"Gemma worked it last year with Joyce, so she'll be a good resource for questions. You can get the program binder from her. She'll be assisting you on-site." His tone held a sense of hesitation, his gaze narrowed with curiosity.

I didn't want him to think I couldn't play nice with coworkers, so I plastered on a perky smile. "Perfect."

I walked out to Gemma's desk and requested the binder.

She slid a massive white binder off the shelf behind her and presented it to me, weighting down my arms. It would be too heavy to lift into an airplane's overhead bin and probably wouldn't fit under the seat in front of me.

"Joyce kept a lot of handwritten notes that aren't in the computer file. She was old school. I hope you'll find everything you need in there." Her devious smile said I wouldn't.

I'd have to come in after hours and empty her shred bin into a garbage bag so Zoe and I could play arts and crafts, gluing all the pages back together.

It was all I could do not to call Rachel and wake her up at 4:00 a.m. to tell her the wench had let her take the fall for her restaurant error. She got up at five, so I called her an hour later and filled her in.

"I screwed up," she said.

"What?"

"After you left me the message, I checked, and I never sent the final payment. I don't know what happened. I've had a hard time focusing lately. I just feel off." She sounded matter-of-fact over having made a fairly big mistake. She used to wig out over one typo in a ten-page meeting agenda.

"Oh well, shit happens."

But it never happened to Rachel.

Even worse, it *hadn't* happened to Gemma.

෧෯ ෯෧

I arrived home a little past six. My shoulder throbbed from the weight of my computer bag, and I couldn't move my wrists after carrying the binder from hell, too big for my bag. Zoe was knitting like a madwoman to replace the half dozen hats Mac had destroyed. Mac was supervising from the floor, giving Zoe his best puppy eyes, but she wasn't caving. She was a stronger woman than me.

She patted the cushion next to her. "Ready for your first knitting lesson?"

"You were serious?" I dropped my computer bag on the floor, and the binder hit the desk with a thud. "I'm never going to be able to learn to knit a dog sweater or a cat hat in a matter of two days."

"Mac said the same thing."

"About me or him?"

Zoe rolled her eyes. "Cheer up. It's the weekend."

"Which I get to cram a twenty-hour online class into, hoping it even touches on hotel contracting."

She popped up from the couch. "I got Chinese takeaway. Kung Pao shrimp, your favorite."

"Awesome. Thank you so much."

Zoe removed the containers from the dorm-size fridge and stuck them in the microwave. I poured two glasses of cabernet in teacups from Grandma's collection, not having yet bought dishes.

I booted up my laptop. "I just have to shoot a quick thank-you to Nicholas Turney. He's going to the registrar's office on Monday to search for my grandma's birth record." I opened my e-mail to find one from a Thomas Ashworth.

Dear Ms. Shaw,

I am contacting you in reference to George Wood, who has become gravely ill. He is currently hospitalized at Lancaster Memorial. I think it best if you are able to pay him a visit as soon as possible. I know how much you mean to him.

Sincerely,
Thomas Ashworth
Head Gardener, The Daly Estate

George was *gravely* ill?

My chest tightened. How could I not go visit him? George had connected with my family thanks to my genealogy research. I'd put him in touch with his paternal aunt Emily Ryan and our cousins Sadie and Seamus. Emily promised to meet up with him when she returned to Dublin from the Canary Islands in April.

And Seamus, at the age of eighty, had never ventured outside Ireland, so he and Sadie had invited George over for a family reunion in June. I'd have to notify them of George's condition.

Were we the only family he had outside of his wife, Diana?

Had he been ill when we'd met last month in Prague? Was he dying? I'd been anxious to visit the Daly Estate, but not under these circumstances.

"What's wrong?" Zoe asked.

"George Wood, my mom's half brother, is really sick."

"What's wrong with him?"

"Not sure. The e-mail is from one of the estate's employees, who says I should go see George in the hospital."

"That's absolutely mad that you have a rellie with an estate. Where 'bouts is he?"

"County Lancashire. A small town in the north."

"Take the ferry. It's probably much cheaper than flying at this late notice, and then you don't have to hire a car. The ferry is lovely. If you haven't drank martinis the night before, out clubbing with the girlies."

"I'm not sure if I get seasick. I've only been on a dinner cruise in Paris and a canoe trip down a river with the Girl Scouts. We had to carry our canoes across land twice, and it took me weeks to get the fiberglass slivers out of my hands."

But my fear over taking a huge ferry, across a huger body of water, ran much deeper than fiberglass slivers in my fingers.

"I have the craft show, or I'd tag along. I need the money. I'll go bonkers if I don't get out of my parents' house."

"Rachel arrives late tomorrow afternoon. I'll wait for her."

"Should you be waiting if the poor bloke is so sick?" Zoe sat down at my laptop and pulled up the ferry schedule. "There's a high-speed one departing at eight a.m., getting into Holyhead, Wales, at ten."

"Wales? How far is that from George?"

Zoe scrunched her forehead. "Two, three hours."

"I can't drive two or three hours to George's. And a high-speed ferry would make me barf for sure."

"A regular ferry is eight hours to Liverpool. Going into Wales, you could bypass Liverpool. Declan could probably catch a flight to Manchester, and you could pick him up there. Maybe Rachel could fly in there also. It's in Lancashire."

"Would Mac be allowed on a ferry?"

Mac let out a bark.

Zoe nodded. "Luckily, I got his passport and vet papers when we'd planned to visit you in the States this spring."

"I can't drive in Dublin or onto a ferry. I get nervous when I have to drive my car into the stall for an oil change, afraid I'm going to drop into the opening in the floor."

"I'd be more worried about the ramp collapsing and the car dropping..." Zoe trailed off, noticing my panicked look. "That only happened once, maybe twice. Very rare. And the drivers survived. You'll be grand."

"Not if I have a heart attack before I hit the water. If I'm afraid to drive in Dublin, I certainly can't drive to Manchester to pick up Declan."

I'd driven twice in Ireland. The first time I'd almost taken out an old man walking his dog. In my defense, he shouldn't have been walking down a narrow road while it was snowing, even in a reflective vest. I then panicked in a roundabout, stalled the car, and was almost rear-ended. The second time I'd only driven a short distance in a rental car before returning it and having Declan take me to the airport Christmas day. Flying alone was one thing. My parents dropped me off at the airport, my flight was usually nonstop, and a car picked me up upon arrival. Taking a ferry when I'd never been on one, sailing across the Irish Sea to an unknown land, then driving hours was beyond terrifying.

Suddenly I was more afraid to drive than to fly!

"Maybe Declan can fly into Dublin early, and then we won't have to worry about it."

I FaceTimed Declan. He was shirtless, changing for an evening event. Picturing him merely in a plaid kilt, I momentarily lost my train of thought.

I gave him the scoop on George's situation. "Can you fly into Dublin earlier and then take the ferry over with me?"

"Afraid not. I'm working VIP ground, and my flight's not until half ten. I could change it to fly into Manchester about the time you'd be driving through."

"How about I fly into Manchester and meet you? We can rent a car there."

"Er, right, then. I'm not really able to rent a car in England. It's a bit of a story."

And undoubtedly a good one. Declan's stories always were.

"Besides, the car rental prices there are mad, dear. You'll be grand. You'll only have to drive to the Manchester airport, and then I'll take over." Noticing my look of sheer panic, he added, "How about I take an Uber to the outskirts and you collect me there?"

I reluctantly agreed since I had little choice.

"I better call my mom. Love you."

I needed to call Mom before contacting Rachel about changing her flight into Manchester instead of Dublin. After all, George was Mom's half brother.

"I'm coming over with Rachel," Mom said. "I should have planned to do that in the first place. George must think I'm an awful person that I was putting it off until summer to come with Teri and Dottie. I just thought the three of us should meet our half brother together. What had I been thinking? I should have at least written to him. I just didn't know what to say. Thank God Teri did. What if he dies and I don't get to meet my only brother?" she rambled on frantically.

Mom had a complete meltdown when I'd told her about George. I feared she was in the middle of another one. If George died only a month after I'd found him, before Mom met him, would she be even more bitter toward her mother?

"Do you want to call Rachel, or should I?" I said.

"I'll call and have her book me on the same flight and add a flight to England. Where do we fly into, and where exactly does George live?"

I gave her the details even though Rachel would be on the phone to me the second their conversation ended.

Mom wasn't only meeting George for the first time but also Declan. She would surely like him. Everyone liked Declan. He was genuinely witty, kind, charming... Everything Andy had pretended to be. Rachel better not have voiced her concern to Mom that Declan was a womanizer and I was setting myself up for the fall. When I'd mentioned approaching Flanagan's for a job, my sister had been worried that I'd quit and move home *when* Declan and I broke up.

I couldn't take off work when I'd only been there for two weeks. I had to finish my online class, figure out how to request proposals from hotels in three countries, finalize two upcoming Dublin meetings, work at my genealogy side job...

What happened to achieving a balanced lifestyle by having a full-time job and not traveling for work? I'd have to return home on Sunday. Mom and Rachel could stay if George was still in the hospital. I had to be to work on Monday. Yet what if George passed away while I was there?

One thing I didn't want to *plan* was my newfound half uncle's funeral.

CHAPTER
FOUR

The Dublin dock area was dark and desolate at six in the morning except for an occasional vehicle on the road or a ship pulling into port. The perfect setting for a major drug deal like in the movies. Several TK Maxx and Tayto semitrailers waiting to be loaded with precious cargo put me slightly at ease. Zoe had dropped me off earlier at Gerry Coffey's townhouse, where Declan parked his car for free. It had only taken me twenty minutes to get to the docks, so now I was driving up and down the roads, surrounded by ship containers and overhead cranes, afraid to sit alone in a parked car. Mac was sleeping peacefully in his purple bed next to me. Must be nice.

About a quarter of a gas tank later, cars started lining up to board the ferry. After presenting my e-ticket and Mac's papers to a ferry employee in a booth, she handed me a boarding card to hang from the rearview mirror. A man in a reflective vest directed me to a designated waiting lane. Before long, my line moved. As I approached the ship, I cringed, trying not to think about the ramp collapsing and my car dropping into the sea. I drove over the ramp, and the metal banged against the pavement. Once safely on board, I turned off the car and set the parking brake, letting out a huge sigh of relief.

One challenge down, a dozen to go.

I slipped a bagel from my purse. An employee approached my car, and I rolled down the window.

"You can't remain in the car, luv," he said.

"Oh, okay." I turned to Mac. "Wake up, pumpkin. We need to go upstairs."

"The little nip needs to stay in the car."

"By himself? He'll freak out."

Snoring away, Mac didn't look the least bit freaked out. He probably wouldn't wake up until we reached Wales.

"He'll be grand. Crack the window. I'll keep an eye on him."

I poured the remainder of my bottled water in Mac's bowl and left a handful of treats, breaking my three-treats-a-day rule. I hiked up a set of metal stairs and entered an interior staircase leading to an upper deck. The ferry certainly wasn't as fancy as a cruise ship, but there was a restaurant, bars, duty-free shopping, video games, and a movie area.

I'd envisioned myself standing on the front deck, my hair blowing back in the wind, like Rose and Jack in the movie *Titanic*. However, passengers were only allowed access to two tiny back corners, one designated smoking.

The ferry pulled away from the dock. I grasped the

handrail, preparing for it to take off like a shot since it was high speed. Yet I could hardly tell we were moving. We cruised alongside other slow-moving boats, obviously a no-wake zone.

My shoulders relaxed. I enjoyed the breathtaking view of Dublin's skyline and the Wicklow Mountains to the south. On my first trip to Ireland, I'd visited County Wicklow, my great-grandma Flannery's homeland. I'd been overwhelmed with a sense of déjà vu. At that moment I knew I belonged in Ireland. I'd never dreamed to one day live here. Despite the difficulties Grandma had endured, I couldn't imagine ever willingly leaving this country.

The ferry was a luxury liner compared to what Grandma had sailed on board. However, same as her, I was traveling to an unknown land, unsure what I would encounter upon my arrival. Too bad she hadn't shared stories about her voyage to America. It'd been too difficult to relive, no doubt. I had a hard time leaving Mac in the car by himself, whereas Grandma had left her son behind. She'd watched England fade into the distance knowing she'd never see him again. My heart ached.

I hadn't judged Grandma for keeping her first husband and supposedly dead family a secret. Yet I was having a difficult time that she'd never told her daughters about their half brother. I better understood Mom's bitterness toward her mother all those years. It was one thing for Mom to never have met her grandparents, but her half brother? Why couldn't Grandma have left a note in her will and given her children the opportunity to connect after her death?

Hopefully, it wouldn't be too late for them to meet.

At least we would be there to comfort George's wife. If she wasn't up to having company, or upset her employee had contacted me, we'd find a hotel. From George's stories, she sounded like a lovely woman. She baked him a weekly loaf of Grandma's brown bread from the recipe I'd e-mailed him. I pictured them eating the bread while sipping tea from Grandma's teacups I'd sent him. A much more positive thought than envisioning George lying ill in a hospital bed.

My hair was whipping against my face, and a chill raced through me. Ireland was quickly fading in the distance behind a long trail of whitecaps and waves. Tucking my hair behind my ears, I walked inside and found a window table to set up a workstation. I needed to get a jump on the incentive trip. I booted up my laptop and connected to the free Wi-Fi. I checked e-mail to find one from Sadie Collentine. She and Seamus were sorry to hear about George, and she was popping a get-well card in the mail. Emily Ryan hadn't yet responded to my news.

I had no clue where to begin checking hotel availability. I shot Mindy, a former coworker, an e-mail asking for recommendations. In Prague she'd mentioned traveling a hundred and fifty days a year. She'd undoubtedly been to Vienna, Florence, and Dubrovnik. And Declan had just done a Florence program, so I could pick his brain. I was a resourceful person. I just couldn't use Rachel as a resource.

I researched whether I could visit any of the three cities if I'd maxed out my ninety-day stay in Ireland before obtaining citizenship. It turned out that Italy and Austria were part of the Schengen Area, which allowed a US citizen to spend ninety days total in any of its twenty-six member countries. Ireland and Croatia weren't members of that area. Croatia would also allow me entry and to stay ninety days.

"Caity Shaw, please proceed to your vehicle on the car deck."

I glanced around, trying to figure out where the announcement was coming from. Why was I being paged to go to my vehicle? Had it gone out of park and hit another car? Had someone hit me? Mac!

I shoved my computer into its bag and raced down the stairs.

The guy who'd directed me to park handed me a puke bag as I headed toward my car. I looked that bad?

"I'm fine," I said.

"The little nip isn't."

I opened the door, and the stench of vomit poured out of the car. I gagged, slapping a hand over my mouth and nose. Mac looked weak, his fur matted with puke. Of course, it was all over Declan's tidy car. I gagged again. How had Mom taken care of Rachel and me all those times we'd been sick?

And here I'd been worried about *me* getting seasick.

❧ ❧

The ferry docked a distance from the terminal, where I stopped to regroup. I cleaned the car the best I could with a T-shirt from my suitcase and antibacterial wipes in my purse. It needed a few air fresheners. Thankfully, Mac wasn't too sick to walk, so I didn't have to carry him into the bathroom to wash him up. I threw away his smelly purple bed and my T-shirt. When I tried to remove his tutu, he growled.

"Don't growl at your mommy."

I tried again.

He growled and swiped a paw at my hand.

Fine. I took back every annoyed thought I'd ever had in stores, restaurants, or movie theaters about mothers being unable to control misbehaving children.

I stuck Mac in the sink and ran warm water. Probably not the most sanitary thing to do, but it was a public bathroom in a ferry terminal, not a fountain in the lobby of the Ritz. I sudsed him up and rinsed him off. I didn't want the car also reeking like wet dog, so I held Mac under the air dryer, warm air blowing against his fur and tutu. He wore a content expression as if enjoying the royal treatment at the doggy spa. A woman and her young daughter walked in and gave me a wary look. I smiled in return.

Fifteen minutes later, we were on a road heading east toward Liverpool. Luckily, it was two lanes on each side, so cars could zip past and I didn't have to worry about driving too slow. Seeing as Declan was forbidden to rent a car in England, I didn't want to lose my license over a speeding ticket I couldn't afford. Yet nobody else seemed worried about a ticket. Maybe my speedometer was off. Sixty seemed awfully slow. The Irish drove faster through roundabouts.

Was England on miles rather than kilometers?

A convenience store or gas station likely sold maps

explaining the road signs. Yet I didn't even own a map for Ireland. I'd winged it the two times I'd driven there.

What if I had to get an Irish license?

I wouldn't be able to wing a driver's test. I'd been so nervous taking my first test I'd almost burst into tears when I had to parallel park. The second time, I'd cussed out a driver who'd pulled out in front of me. It'd taken me three tries to get my license. A good thing I could rely on mass transportation in Dublin. However, my dream was to live in a rural area nearer to Declan's parents in Glenteen and Grandma's hometown, Killybog.

I'd have to learn to drive a tractor.

Mac pawed at the window, whimpering for me to open it farther than the crack at the top. He strained his neck, trying to stick his nose out for fresh air.

"I am not opening the window so you can jump out on the freeway, so deal with the smell. I am."

I took a whiff of fresh air whenever I dared take my eyes off the road for a second.

We left behind gorgeous ocean views and wide sandy beaches for a landscape with red-tiled roofs and brick buildings surrounded by fields of sheep and cattle.

An hour later I was starting to feel a false sense of confidence when the GPS directed me onto a six-lane motorway. Cars flew by me. My grip tightened on the steering wheel. I was so overwhelmed by signs for the Liverpool airport, city center, and Manchester I didn't see the signs for construction. Traffic came to a screeching halt, and I almost slammed into a black Mercedes. The guy in a Beemer behind me laid on his horn. Mac let out a bark and jumped into the backseat, barking ferociously at the driver.

The road narrowed to two congested lanes, and I was driving dangerously close to a cement barrier. I'd be taking the first exit off the highway from hell.

According to the GPS, Manchester airport was an hour away, which would be a couple-hundred-dollar Uber ride. Ugh. I had to do this. I could do this.

Mac was now howling at the car.

I questioned my desire to have children.

⁂

Mac and I let out a humongous sigh of relief when I pulled off the motorway into a rest stop. I also let out a nervous giggle, trying to relax my death grip on the steering wheel. Put a TK Maxx here and I might make a weekend of it. There was a hotel with an indoor swimming pool next to a complex with small shops, a Burger King and other chain restaurants, an M & S Food Market, and a coffee shop.

Mac was perched on the edge of the seat, his tail wagging at the sight of a large stretch of grass and a plastic bag dispenser with a dog's picture. His tail slapped frantically against the car door when he spotted Declan in front of the main building, wearing his black-and-green plaid kilt and black shirt. Mac barked, and I about howled. Maybe I shouldn't rip on the poor dog for being obsessed with his tutu. Maybe he thought it was a kilt and was proud of his Irish heritage.

I was so distracted by Declan's insanely sexy legs that I forgot to downshift, and the car rocked to a halt. Thankfully, I was in a parking spot this time. I flew from the car, Mac hot on my heels. I flung my arms around Declan's neck and kissed him senseless. He smelled like freshly fallen rain and woodsy cologne and tasted like fries. My stomach growled. Declan curled his fingers into the back of my cream wool sweater and pressed my body against his. I let out a moan and Mac barked, pawing at us for attention. I reluctantly drew back, sharing Declan with him.

"Are you wearing anything under that kilt?" I said in a breathless, flirty tone.

"Didn't think I was still *wearing* it after that welcome." The corners of his lips curled into a sly smile.

I glanced over at the hotel. "You don't have to be."

A mischievous glint twinkled in his dreamy blue eyes. "We should probably be calling on George during visiting hours."

I nodded, having momentarily forgotten my worries.

Declan eyed Mac's tutu. "Still celebrating, are ya?"

"Won't let me take it off. I'm going to take him to the potty. Can you grab me a Whopper and see if the convenience store has air fresheners. Like a half dozen."

Declan arched a curious brow, opening the hatchback to stick in his suitcase. His top lip curled back. "Jaysus, what the hell happened in here?"

"Mac got seasick."

"Hope I won't be getting carsick. That's wretched." He tossed his suitcase in the back and slammed the door.

Five minutes later, we met Declan back at the car, hanging a raspberry-scented air freshener from the rearview mirror and tossing a lemon-scented one in the backseat.

Curled up on my lap, Mac peered over at Declan with soft brown eyes, still looking a bit peaked. His confrontation with the Beemer earlier had drained him.

Declan gave the top of his head a rub. "Ah, you'll be grand, little fella."

I enjoyed a Whopper and the fact that Declan was behind the wheel now instead of me. Mac didn't even bark for a bite, still under the weather.

"My mom decided to come over with Rachel to visit George. They're flying into Dublin today and catching an Aer Lingus flight to Manchester tonight."

Declan's smile failed to hide the nervous twitch at the corners of his mouth. "That's brilliant."

"Then why do you look freaked out? Like I'm behind the wheel driving right now?"

Declan was usually the one who remained calm in any situation, while I flipped out.

He shrugged faintly. "Not a' tall. I'll finally have the chance to meet your mum."

"Don't worry. She doesn't blame you for her daughter moving four thousand miles away from home." I gave him a teasing smile.

"Gee, thanks a mil."

"She's going to love you. She can be a bit overbearing and nosy, but she means well. You'll be a prince compared to Andy."

Declan had learned about my ex when I'd pepper sprayed him in Dublin, fearing he was Andy. And after that I'd wigged out on him a few times before eventually opening up about my emotionally abusive relationship. Random smells, sounds, or people's actions reminding me of my ex were becoming rarer and rarer.

I lived for the day they were nonexistent.

"So why can't you rent a car in England?"

"Bloody car hire companies blacklisted me. Consider me a high risk."

I nodded. "I used to consider you a high risk."

When we'd met, Declan had a bit of a womanizer reputation. Once I got to know him, I realized it was a survival tactic so he wouldn't become emotionally attached to a woman after his wife's death. Thankfully, I'd ignored Rachel's warnings and discovered the real Declan for myself.

He gave me a sly smile. "I've had two rental cars nicked here. The car hires were starting to think I had a theft ring, even though I found the one Peter had hidden and returned it. The agent wasn't happy we'd been too knackered to clean out the streams of toilet paper after a mate's bachelor party in Liverpool."

"What about the second car?"

He shrugged. "Never found it."

"I can't wait to meet Peter's girlfriend, Charlotte."

The woman who'd been able to tame Peter Molloy's wild ways. I'd met the owner of Molloy's pub at Christmastime. He'd helped me connect with my rellies Sadie and Seamus.

"She undoubtedly has a lot of interesting stories about you guys. I bet she and I will be great friends."

Declan quirked a brow. "That's what I'm afraid of."

CHAPTER FIVE

George lived near Dalwick, a village bordering northern Lancashire and Yorkshire counties. The closest hospital was in Lancaster—a lively college town filled with heavy pedestrian traffic, stone buildings, and quaint shops. A medieval castle sat atop a hill. Sadly, we were there to visit a modern hospital constructed of concrete and glass, not a historical stone fortress.

We walked up to a young nurse in a pink uniform at the reception desk and inquired about George.

"Are you a relative?" she asked.

I nodded. "He's my uncle." I wasn't sure if *half* uncle would allow me visitation rights.

The woman glanced over at her coworker, who nodded. "She's the only family member who's been here to see him."

That about made me burst into tears.

"His wife, Diana, isn't here?" I asked.

The two women exchanged glances.

"He has a wife?" the one asked the other.

"Does who have a wife?" an older nurse asked, walking up.

"George Wood."

She shook her head, snatching a file from a shelf. "She's been gone several years." She whisked off.

The nurse in pink gave me a curious stare. *How hadn't I known this if he was my uncle?*

"I haven't visited in a while."

She gave us the room number and allowed Mac to join us as long as we only stayed a few minutes. Declan slipped his hand around mine and led me down the hallway in a daze, Mac trotting on a leash in front of us.

"Why did George lie about his wife being alive? She'd supposedly baked him my grandma's Irish brown bread. He'd said it was the most delicious bread he'd ever had. That they'd drank tea from my grandma's cups I'd sent him. Is he even really my grandma's son? Maybe in his baptism picture Grandma and Michael had been godparents like I'd originally thought. Rachel had questioned his claim from the start. I never had."

"In all fairness to George, not being up front about his wife having passed doesn't mean he's lying about everything. It's tough losing a spouse."

But Declan had never lied, claiming Shauna was alive. He merely hadn't told me he'd had a wife until we were working our second meeting together, in Paris.

"Might be healthier than not talking about her a' tall. It was fiercely difficult for me to discuss Shauna. It became easier to just not talk about her period. Lucky to have found love again. Hopefully, George will." Declan brushed a kiss across my lips and gave my hand an encouraging squeeze.

We entered George's room. Beeping monitors and a wheezing sound came from behind the white privacy curtain. I peeked cautiously around the curtain at a thin, pale man with an oxygen mask over his mouth and an IV in his arm. He looked nothing like the cheery George I'd met at the trendy lounge in Prague. My eyes watered from the memories of our first visit...and the overpowering scent of flowers. Purple pom-poms, yellow daffodils, and pink peonies filled vases lining the windowsill, desk, and nightstand.

Shaken by George's fragile appearance, I occupied myself with a vase of colorful tulips. The card read *Get well soon. Fanny.* I snapped my hand back, realizing I was invading George's privacy. He probably hadn't even read his cards.

Mac hopped up on the bed, coming dangerously close to the IV line entering George's lower arm. George didn't even flinch. Declan snatched the dog off the bed seconds before a nurse walked in.

"Is he in a coma?" I asked her.

I'd been so stunned upon discovering George's wife had died I hadn't inquired about his condition.

She shook her head. "He's quite weak from the pneumonia and is heavily medicated. Is out most of the time. Came to for a bit last night but wasn't coherent. The fluid in his lungs is a concern. If the issue doesn't resolve itself soon, we'll have to insert a catheter and drain it."

I grasped hold of Declan's arm, feeling light-headed at the thought of the procedure. "Would he have to be put down for that?"

The nurse looked baffled and a bit mortified.

"Ah, she meant put *under*," Declan said.

"Oh, God yeah, put under. Sorry. I was thinking about my cat when...never mind."

The nurse nodded faintly. "Merely a local anesthetic." She gave us a sympathetic smile but no reassurance that George would be up and walking around in no time at all. She left.

"At least he doesn't have to be put under," I said. "That'd probably be risky at his age. When my cat Izzy was fifteen, she had to be put under for bladder stone surgery, and she had a reaction. They had to put her down."

I sucked in a calming breath, needing to be strong in case George could hear us. If he could, I didn't want to mention that Mom and Rachel were coming. That might make him think he was in really bad shape.

Which it sounded like he was.

⁊❧ ❦⁊

I input George's address in the GPS, and we headed toward his house. We rounded a corner on a one-lane country road and encountered a half dozen sheep munching on shrubs lining the sides of the narrow road. Unfazed by our arrival, they continued dining. Declan honked the horn. Their ears shot back, and one gave us an annoyed glance, then went back to eating. If I were able to open the door, I'd hop out and shoo them up the road. The sheep trotted for a short distance, then stopped for dessert.

Fifteen minutes later, we came upon a black iron

gate with a plaque set in a stone wall that read *Daly Estate*. A tingle of excitement raised the hairs on my arms. Declan opened the unlocked gate without triggering an alarm. I glanced up at the surveillance camera as a sheep ran toward the gate. Declan darted in its path, blocking the entrance. I placed Mac on the seat and jumped out. I distracted the determined animal while Declan drove in. Mac was now awake and barking up a storm. I quickly closed the gate behind us. I flashed the sheep a victorious grin, then glanced up at the security camera.

That video clip had better not show up on social media.

We headed down a tree-lined gravel drive. Fields gave way to mowed grass and yellow daffodils. Shrubs in the shape of dogs appeared to be running alongside us, escorting us to the house.

"The head gardener, Thomas Ashworth, must have quite the landscaping team," I said.

At the end of the drive, a shrub resembling a man towered over one side, a woman on the other. Her breasts and every curve of her body trimmed to perfection. My gaze narrowed on the man's private parts.

"Are those nudes?" I said.

"The *Venus de Milo* and *David*."

"They must be good if you can recognize them in the form of shrubs. But seems kind of risqué for a proper English estate."

"It's art. Quite good, it is."

We parked in the circular drive in front of a red brick mansion. The home looked the same as in the picture George had given me. Except bigger. I sucked at gauging square footage, but my parents' ranch was sixteen hundred square feet, and about seven or eight of my family's home could fit in this one. Yet two or three of this mansion would fit inside Downton Abbey. Huge was relative.

I stepped from the car and set Mac on the ground. "I can't believe my grandma and her husband once lived here. They probably held garden parties under large white tents and played cricket on the lawn."

"The house is a wee bit bigger than your granny's cottage in Ireland, I'd say."

It was bigger than the Daly Estate up the hill from Grandma's family home in Ireland, where the Dalys had looked down on the Coffeys, disowning their son for marrying one.

Five months ago I'd visited my first castle, Malahide Castle near Dublin. This wasn't as grand, but it was impressive enough to be a historic stately home on my long bucket list. Yet I wasn't in the mood for playing tourist, having my pic taken in front of the house. I wanted to step back in time and take it all in, as Grandma likely had when she and Michael strolled up the drive over eighty years ago, hand in hand. They'd undoubtedly been anxious to embark on their new life together, unaware that Michael's would sadly end just two years later.

Closed red drapes hung in the white lattice-framed windows. Mac sniffed a purple lilac bush. He'd recently used the doggie rest stop, so rather than doing his duty, he plopped down in the sun next to the bush. I didn't want the lingering smell of puke to be everyone's first impression of us, so I tied Mac's leash to an iron pole near the front door.

Declan gave my hand a reassuring squeeze. I inhaled a shaky breath and rang the doorbell next to the massive wooden door. My heart raced with anticipation. I hoped the interior was reminiscent of Grandma's era and hadn't been modernized with large-screen TVs in the den and a shiny stainless-steel kitchen.

I rang the doorbell again. "I can't imagine nobody is here, unless we missed them at the hospital. There's surely a housekeeper and a cook, since his wife passed away, and Thomas, the head gardener. The gate wouldn't be open if nobody was home. Right?"

I clanked the iron door knocker against the solid wood. As if that would be louder than the doorbell.

Declan turned the brass knob, and the door clicked open.

I grasped hold of his arm. "We can't just walk in."

"Why not? George said it's your place as much as his."

I bit down on my lip in contemplation. "Yeah, but still..."

Declan opened the creaking door wider. "Hello," he called out, poking his head inside. He paused a moment before withdrawing and closing the door, wearing an uneasy smile. "Right, then, probably rude to just be letting ourselves in."

Why the sudden hesitation?

My curiosity trumped proper etiquette.

I opened the door and stepped into a small foyer. A shiver shot through me from the cold temperature and dreary atmosphere. I walked into the salon, peering around in shock. "Omigod..."

My voice echoed off the bare hardwood floor and through the empty room, up a wooden staircase to the second floor. At the top landing, a yellow-and-red stained-glass window allowed sunshine to filter in through a dirty film. A vase of yellow daffodils sat in the windowsill, trying its hardest to perk up the room and camouflage the musty smell. Bright areas of red paint, where artwork or wall décor once hung, broke up the faded walls, as did meandering cracks in the plaster. A lonely painting hung over the fireplace—a refined-looking couple and young boy in front of a Christmas tree. George and his adoptive parents? The stern-looking man reminded me of the portrait at the Daly's home in Killybog, Ireland, but not quite as scary.

"Was the place robbed while George has been in the hospital?" I said.

"The staff and neighbors would surely have noticed lorries clearing out the salon."

I looked around. "What staff?" I gestured to a set of freshly cut scratches and grooves across the dark wooden floor. "Whoever hauled stuff out didn't give a rip about the floors."

"Maybe he was in the middle of moving when he became ill."

"We e-mail several times a week. Why wouldn't he have told me he was moving from a home that had been in his family for generations? What he planned to do when Rachel and I visited next week?"

I tried not to be upset when George was lying in a hospital bed fighting for his life. Yet I was hurt that he hadn't confided in me about the estate or his wife.

I walked across the foyer. Even the squeak from my rubber-soled shoes echoed faintly through the room. Framed photos of George's family and mine mingled on the fireplace's wooden mantel. A large vase of pink peonies sat on each end.

I shook my head in disbelief as we continued through a wide doorway leading into a library. The built-in bookcases—void of books—almost reached the high oak-paneled ceiling. One scarred shelf displayed recent and vintage family photos and floral bouquets in empty wine bottles and clear jars. The home's vases were likely all in George's hospital room with peonies, daffodils, and pom-poms. I frowned. Had all the flowers come from the estate except for Fanny's tulips?

A worn red velvet couch and a cocktail table sat in front of the marble fireplace. An antique desk with a fancy inlaid wood design and leather upholstered chair faced a tall curtainless window. The wavy glass provided a distorted yet breathtaking view of the colorful gardens. I fought the urge to throw open a window and let the musty air out and some warmth and sunshine in.

In the next room, a small occasional table with two chairs sat in the center of a large formal dining area with yellow walls and white crown molding.

Declan eyed three crystal decanters on the table, containing gold- and brown-colored liquors. "Good man."

I was more interested in the silver teapot next to the decanters and Grandma's three cups I'd sent George. Hopefully, I wouldn't be taking them back to Ireland with me. At the end of the room, Declan opened a white door leading to the kitchen. I gasped, startled at the sight of an older man at a massive cast-iron stove.

The short man raised a frying pan with both hands. Besides the fact that he struggled to keep the iron pan in the air, his wide-brimmed straw hat, yellow wellies, and floral apron made him appear quite harmless.

"What the bloody hell are you doing here? House isn't for sale yet. Now get out before I call the police and have you arrested for trespassing." He attempted to shake the pan at us, grimacing as if the weight might break his wrists.

"Not here to buy the place," Declan said. "We came to visit George Wood in the hospital."

"Are you Thomas Ashworth?" I asked.

The man's weathered features relaxed, and he nodded faintly, lowering the pan. He wasn't exactly what I'd expected from such a regal-sounding name. Not that dressy wool pants, a tweed jacket, and riding boots would be practical attire for a gardener, but that was how I'd envisioned him.

"I'm Caity Shaw. You e-mailed me."

A sense of relief washed over his face. "Caity Shaw. Why, I'm so glad you came." He removed his straw hat. "Please excuse my lack of manners. Thought George's greedy cousin or that annoying fella from the bank was sending over more prospective buyers. That man's poor mother would turn over in her grave if she knew he was beating down doors bullying money out of the respectable people she'd known her entire life."

Ignoring bills and past-due notices didn't make them go away. Bill collectors were quite persistent. Like sending a repo company to steal your sporty red car right from in front of your house while your mom was eating breakfast.

"So the house is going up for sale?" I asked. "Where's George living?"

"Hasn't moved anywhere yet."

"Where are all the furnishings?"

Thomas heaved a sigh, dropping down in a chair at a small wooden table. "Has sold most everything off to pay bills, yet still owes."

Why hadn't George asked us for help? Because he'd contacted us for moral support, not financial. According to the nurse, no family had been to visit him. My family, Emily Ryan, Sadie, and Seamus were likely the only living relatives to help him through these tough times. It didn't sound like he could rely on support from his greedy cousins.

"What will he do when the place sells? Where will he go?"

Thomas shrugged faintly, looking too depressed about it to even lift his shoulders.

A teakettle whistled on the stove.

The gardener went to stand, and I placed a comforting hand on his shoulder. "I'll get it."

He gave me an appreciative smile.

The cupboard contained a full set of china—a bluish green with fancy gold scrollwork and yellow roses. George had mentioned he would reciprocate my kindness for sending him Grandma's teacups with one from the Daly's china collection.

Thankfully, it was still intact.

I poured hot water into a china teapot and added several tea bags. I placed three cups and saucers on the table, along with a plate of sliced bread and a small bowl of jam sitting on the counter.

"The china is one of the only things George hasn't been able to bring himself to sell. It's been in the Daly family for generations. Same as my family. My father was the head gardener before me, and his father before him. I grew up in the cottage down the dirt road just inside the entrance. Will remain there until someone buys the place and evicts me."

I poured tea, then sat next to Thomas.

"It's a historic home," Declan said. "Any chance George could be getting government funding or a national trust to help him out?"

Thomas shook his head. "England has many country homes in need of assistance. And the house had to be open to the public for inheritance taxes to be waived. George is probably still paying on those. After the theft, George's parents refused to open the front door for friends, let alone strangers."

"What theft?" I asked.

Thomas's blue eyes dimmed. "In 1993. Four blokes rang the doorbell and forced their way into the house. Stole over ten million pounds in artwork."

Ten *million* pounds? I considered Declan's Christmas painting and sketch of me as priceless works of art, yet they might be worth a hundred bucks. I couldn't imagine having such valuable artwork hanging on my walls.

"Weren't they insured?" As if I had a clue about insuring priceless artwork. I was still looking into affordable health insurance.

He nodded. "Not sure exactly how they fared, as the alarm wasn't set. After the theft, Mr. Wood Senior donated some of the more valuable paintings to the Tate museum, wanting them safe even though the new security system was impenetrable."

"Pretty ballsy thieves waltzing in and walking off with such valuable artwork," I said.

"Happens more than you'd think, even in high security facilities," Declan said. "Not long ago a Paris museum was robbed while the guards slept, and alarms didn't go off. Some bloke accessed the Van Gogh Museum with a ladder, breaking in through a window."

"A car drove through the patio doors of a Scotland home not long ago and made off with millions in artwork," Thomas said.

"Did they ever catch the thieves here?" I asked.

The gardener shook his head, rubbing a hand over his stubbly chin. "Not long after that, the family needed funds for repairs, but George's mother feared if the house was open to the public, people would steal even more. Now, if it was donated to the National Trust, George may be able to remain in residence, but the place isn't so big that he could close off a private wing. Even if George could afford to donate it rather than selling it, the National Trust likely wouldn't accept it with all the needed repairs. Not like Queen Victoria slept in the master bedroom. No real historical significance attached to the home. George's grandfather, Arthur Daly, bought it in the 1860s with the fortune he'd made from coal and iron." Thomas slathered berry jam on a slice of bread and took a bite.

I shook my head in dismay, trying to process

everything. "I'm so sorry if I wasn't clear in my e-mail that we were coming today. It was all just so sudden. I didn't even have the chance to make reservations. Is there a hotel or B and B nearby we can stay at?"

"Nonsense. George would insist you stay here. There are several bedrooms upstairs."

With beds?

I took a bite of bread. The familiar taste of the moist dense bread with a crumbly crust brought back memories of Grandma's sunny-yellow kitchen filled with the scent of fresh-baked goods. "Just like my grandma used to make." Mom had made it for the first time in years this past Christmas.

"I bake George a loaf every week. I've been bringing him some in the hospital."

Rather than George's *wife* having baked it as he'd claimed.

"When did Diana pass away?"

"The bloody wench died? Alleluia." Thomas made the sign of the cross. "May she rot in hell."

Um, how hadn't Thomas known she'd died if he worked and lived on the estate?

"Sorry. When the nurse said she'd been *gone* several years, I'd assumed she'd died."

The man's smile faded. "My apologies. My enthusiasm over her death must seem quite inappropriate, but I never cared for the woman. None of us did, except George. She somehow had him fooled until after his mother's death, when she ran off with the bank account and the family's solicitor. George had considered opening the house to the public to pay for repairs. Diana panicked that she'd lose her place in society once people learned the estate was in ruins. He became quite depressed and never pursued the possibility of opening the house, claiming he was honoring his mother's wishes.

"Diana was greedy like his cousins, who assumed George would leave them the estate as he didn't have an heir. They were livid when they learned the place is going on the market. Where were they when the roof needed repairs and the electrical rewiring? You know what insurance alone costs on a place like this? The demise of the estate began with the art theft, and that bloody woman took what little they had left."

A loud bark brought Thomas to his feet.

"Sorry. That's our dog, Mac."

Our dog?

Declan quirked an intrigued brow.

Another bark, and I stood. "I should check on him."

Thomas smiled. "Will be nice to have a dog around. Haven't had one since Diana ran off with Freddie, their cocker spaniel."

Wretched woman! Diana running off with George's dog was even more unforgivable than her stealing his money.

We walked outside to find Mac sitting in a bed of flattened flowers.

My gaze darted to Thomas. "I'm so sorry."

"No worries. She's a precious little thing." He gave Mac a pat. "What's her name?"

"Mac. It's a he."

Damn tutu.

"Naughty," I scolded Mac. "Why can't you be more like Esmé?"

I suddenly realized I'd been comparing Mac to Esmé a lot lately. Same as how Mom used to compare me to Rachel. *Why can't your grades be as good as your sister's? Why can't you keep your room clean like your sister's?* So I'd been shocked when Mom had recently told me she feared I *was* becoming like Rachel, losing my fun-loving spirit and turning into a stressed-out workaholic. I gave Mac a pat on the head, apologizing for being one of *those* mothers.

Declan grabbed the suitcases from the car, and Thomas led us up the staircase to the second floor. I imagined elegantly dressed women sashaying down the stairs, making a grand entrance to greet dinner guests. When we reached the top, I paused and took in the view below, picturing the empty walls filled with artwork, the floor with antique furnishings. How sad.

The long hallway was dark until Thomas opened the second door and sunshine poured through the curtainless windows. A thick crack ran across the blue wall from the hardwood floor to the white crown molding. A brown water stain had caused the white ceiling paint to peel, and pieces of paint and plaster had dropped to the floor, landing next to a silver bucket waiting to catch water. Being in England, the chance for rain was quite good. I'd have to keep an eye on that bucket.

The room was the size of my apartment. A faded oil painting of the estate hung on the wall over the head of a four-poster bed with a blue quilt. A wooden rocking horse sat in a corner. It reminded me of My Little Pony and the toys Mom had thankfully boxed up and stored in the basement despite me insisting she could give them to charity. I pictured Grandma rocking George to sleep in the wooden chair, with a blue afghan draped over the back. My eyes watered.

"I'll just need to change the bedding," Thomas said.

"If you give us the sheets, we'll take care of that."

"First I'll get some heat going." He bent down and turned the knob on the rusted cast-iron wall radiator.

I tried to stop shivering so he wouldn't feel the need to heat the place on my behalf. I gestured to the fireplace. "A fire is fine."

"You'll need a bit of heat when you wake up in the morning."

"I don't want to run up the fuel bill." It likely cost a fortune just to heat this room. "My mom always kept the thermostat low, and if we complained, she'd tell us to put on a sweater." But Rachel was a wimp. She'd freeze her butt off here.

"I'll keep it low." He gave me a wink. "Besides, a bit of heat helps remove the dampness."

Setting this room on *fire* couldn't get rid of the dampness.

Declan set down my suitcase. "Another room close by, is there?"

I shot him a baffled look.

"We aren't sleeping together with your mum here."

"I'm a grown woman. If I want to sleep with you, I will. She's not that naïve. She knows we sleep together."

I'd made the mature decision that I was being open and honest with Mom about my relationship with Declan, unlike everything I'd hidden from her about Andy.

"Not with her right in the house, we don't."

Thomas cleared his throat, looking embarrassed by our conversation. "We have two more furnished bedrooms. George couldn't bear to see his parents' rooms cleaned out."

Parents' *rooms*? They hadn't slept together?

"I guess I'll be sharing a bed with Rachel."

Declan's nervousness over meeting my mom was quickly going from endearing to annoying. But I wasn't going to argue about it further in front of poor Thomas. He led Declan to his room.

I swept a hand over the wooden rocking horse. Had losing the family estate caused George to lose his will to live? Was that why he'd succumbed to pneumonia? That and the cold, damp house? He'd spent his entire life on the Daly Estate. He should be able to die here. The place was part of George's identity, part of who he was. I could tell by the way he talked about it. George being evicted from the Daly Estate would be like me being deported from Ireland. It had taken me twenty-four years to find my place in the world.

With a bit of luck, maybe we'd both end up being able to live where we belonged.

CHAPTER SIX

Mac and I waited outside for Declan so we could head into Dalwick for groceries. We couldn't all survive on Grandma's delicious brown bread. The dog attempted to detour toward the lilac shrubs and flowerbed. "You've done enough damage." I directed him over to the *Venus de Milo*, where Thomas was pruning some stray leaves and twigs from her curvy figure.

"That is absolutely incredible," I said, admiring the shrub. "How long did it take to design?"

"Almost five years. It's actually two shrubs grown together, framed, and trained to grow up and mature to the point of shaping. It requires a frequent prune here and there."

"Did you go to school for it?"

"A family trade. Passed down from my grandfather. My topiary has won several awards and been featured in numerous magazines." Thomas wore a proud look, gazing longingly at his work of art. His smile faded. "That was before the theft. Now, I do it more for the relaxation than the recognition." His somber tone said he'd welcome the attention if he were once again permitted to show his shrubs.

Declan walked out the front door.

"We'll be back in a bit," I said.

"You can leave the little fella here if you'd like. Be nice to have the company."

"Are you sure?"

He gave Mac a pat on the head. "You can be my apprentice."

Surprisingly, Mac sat, agreeing to stay. Behaving was another thing. I shot him a warning look that he better not be naughty. I joined Declan, eyeing his jeans with disapproval. Not that his butt didn't look incredible in a pair of Levi's, but he wore jeans all the time.

"Where's the kilt?"

"A bit cool for a kilt, I'd say. And it's absolutely bitter inside the house."

"You're from Ireland. Suck it up and put the skirt back on."

Declan's gaze narrowed. "A *skirt*, ya say?"

"Sorry. Put the *kilt* back on."

He gestured to my sweater. "While you're wearing a wool jumper?"

"I'm not first-generation Irish."

"You're from Wisconsin."

I let out a defeated sigh, heading over to the car. "I wish there was something we could do to help George, but I might be in worse financial shape than he is."

"He'll make a load of quid off the sale of the estate even if it needs repairs. Too bad he couldn't get a TV show to film here. He'd be grand. There's a castle near my parents' that rents haunted rooms to ghost-hunter shows or anyone willing to pay the price"—Declan waggled his fingers in a mysterious manner—"and stay the night."

I peered at the vacant upstairs windows, and a chill slithered up my spine. "This place better not be haunted after I just stayed at one of the most haunted hotels in the world, in Prague."

"I went to a music festival at that castle a few years ago. They need to be creative to keep the place going."

"I wouldn't have a clue how to arrange a music fest. And I think poor Thomas would have a stroke when people trampled through his gardens and flowerbeds at Woodstock UK."

"Also attended a mate's wedding there. These grounds would make a brilliant wedding venue if it weren't March."

"Would give Thomas the chance to show off his shrubs. But you heard what he said. George refuses to open the place up to the public, and you certainly can't rely on England's weather to hold all events outdoors." I let out a depressed sigh. "Let's go buy groceries and some lottery tickets."

❧ ☙

Dalwick was a picture-postcard village. If it wasn't in a tourism brochure, it should be. Ivy and lush foliage covered a stone bridge spanning across a gurgling river where two young boys were attempting to skip rocks across the moving water. Red and green wooden benches encouraged people to enjoy the view from the grassy banks. A fancy iron scrollwork sign advertised a busy café housed in a stone building next to Nicole's Vintage Finds. Nicole's *finds* had found their way from the shop onto the patch of grass in front. Speckled with water spots and traces of dirt, the teacups and saucers, dessert plates, and serving dishes had apparently been outside more than a night.

Clear packaging tape paired matching teacups and saucers, while mismatched ones filled bins, allowing people to piece together their own sets. I checked the bottom of several cups, finding them all made in England rather than at my Flannery rellies' factory in County Wicklow. I chose a pink set with an English cottage design. A steal for three pounds.

"I must have this." It would be a nice addition to my quickly growing teacup collection. I walked over to the shop. A closed sign hung on the door. "Crap."

"Can pay on your honor." Declan pointed to a weathered wooden box by the door for depositing payments.

"Wow, pretty trusting." I dropped coins in the box.

"Small town."

We strolled hand in hand down the narrow road, encountering a shop window displaying an oil painting of the town's bridge and river.

"Let's give it a look," Declan said.

It was a positive sign that he was still showing an interest in art. Declan sketching me in Prague had been a big step forward in our relationship. He hadn't drawn or painted since Shauna's death three years ago.

We popped inside the gallery where a refined-looking woman—thirtyish, in a pink sheath dress, dark hair pulled up on top of her head—was talking to an older couple in casual clothing. She gave us a smile and continued their conversation.

The painting in the window cost five hundred pounds.

"Yikes, that's out of my budget."

"*That* attitude is precisely why I could never make a living painting. The artist likely spent several days, or weeks, creating an original such as that. Not much of a wage, I'd say. Yet buyers still think it's too dear."

"I'm sure it's worth the price. I just couldn't afford it." As I walked out, my gaze narrowed on a flyer by the door advertising a countywide art festival with a gallery hop, including this one. "Too bad we won't be here in two weeks."

The flyer highlighted a local castle opening to the public for the occasion. Like the Ireland castle Declan had mentioned, which held special events to stay afloat...

"What if we *were* here in two weeks? What if we coincided an event at George's with this art festival?" My mind raced with ideas. "Like incorporating the estate's art theft slant? Mindy mentioned in Prague that her client does murder-mystery dinners. What if we did one where people have to solve the art theft? Maybe someone would miraculously solve the crime for real. Crack a cold case."

Declan's lips curled into a teasing smile. "Moving up from finding stolen macaroons to stolen artwork, are ya? That would bring a bit of media attention to the estate and attract visitors."

Actually, I hadn't *found* the macaroons in Prague. They'd found me. The thief had panicked over possibly getting caught and returned them to the hotel's cooler. Yet I'd caught the thief. Thanks to sheer luck.

"You could paint reproductions of the stolen artwork to hang on the walls"—I framed the air with my hands, setting the scene—"and then several go missing. Who took them? Yet that'd be a lot of paintings to crank out in two weeks."

I wasn't sure if Declan was prepared for such an extensive endeavor. It would be nice for him to keep up the momentum. To reignite the passion he'd once had, using his natural talent.

He nodded. "I could easily paint two a day."

"A *day*?"

"I'm a bit rusty. A great forger can crank out a Monet in a few hours. *I'm* not a forger, but the paintings wouldn't have to be perfect. Nobody would be knowing the difference."

"You could paint fakes for people to buy as souvenirs. Art buffs would go wild over a fake stolen painting. Is that legal to paint masterpieces and sell them? I don't want you getting banned from England by more than car rental agencies."

"It's legal unless I try to pass them off as the real thing."

The couple who'd been chatting with the saleswoman walked out, and she offered us assistance.

"Would you know how we could get in touch with the person in charge of the festival?" Declan asked.

She nodded, walking over to her desk. "Are you interested in participating? Do you run a gallery?"

"The Daly Estate might be," Declan said.

She arched a perfect brow. "Really?" She handed him a business card for the festival's organizer. "The Daly house would definitely be a draw. The place has quite a mysterious reputation. Locals would be curious to peek inside. I'd be curious to see their art collection."

It was a bit late for that.

"None of the stolen paintings ever showed up on the black market?" Declan asked.

"Not that I ever heard. I was quite young when the theft occurred."

"Would be difficult for a thief to legitimately sell the paintings without a provenance, and fabricating one would be more difficult than the theft itself," Declan said.

"You should check old newspapers at the library. I'm sure you could find articles on it."

We thanked her and left.

"If I order art supplies online, I could have them overnighted," Declan said. "Framing is dear. Could just do canvases. Like she said, people will be curious to peek inside the house. Won't be caring if the paintings are framed or not."

"Yeah, people would be nosing around, talking about the empty house that once held a pricey art collection. I don't want George to be embarrassed about having sold everything off. Maybe we should wait until we can talk to him so he can okay the idea. Maybe he'll be better soon. I have no right going against his wish of not opening to the public." Reality burst my bubble. I let out a frustrated groan.

"What does he have to lose at this point? There's nothing left in the house to nick. Opening the house up to the public would be better than selling it."

"I have *George* to lose. Going against his wishes and upsetting him might be the end of our relationship."

I didn't want to lose him.

Not after he'd just found me.

CHAPTER SEVEN

When we returned to the house, Thomas had finished pruning his artwork, and Mac was lying next to the lilac bush. An elderly woman in a light-blue coat and square-heeled cream shoes was walking across the circular drive. A large wicker basket in her hand weighted down one side of her petite frame. Declan and I gave her a wave and parked. Declan relieved her of the basket containing the scent of something delish, and I untied Mac's leash from the pole by the door.

"Hello there," she said, brushing a white-gloved hand across Mac's back. She peered over at us. "What's her name?"

"Mac," I said, not bothering to explain that *he* was merely obsessed with his tutu.

She eyed us with curiosity. "I'm Fanny, Fanny Bing."

The woman who'd left the tulips in George's hospital room.

We introduced ourselves.

A glint of recognition shown in Fanny's pale-blue

eyes, which matched the faint blue tint in her gray hair. She smiled. "How nice you came to visit George. He'll be so pleased."

George had obviously mentioned me, but had he mentioned how we were related?

"I brought some fresh-baked scones, if someone will be paying him a visit this evening or in the morning. I won't be able to call on him until tomorrow afternoon." She drew back the corner of a floral linen, offering a peek at some yummy-looking baked goods.

My stomach growled.

Declan smiled. "They look grand. We'll be sure he gets them."

"I made his favorite, strawberry with little chocolate chips. Tastes like chocolate-covered strawberries. There's plenty. You must try one. My friends and I are holding a church bake sale. Every penny helps." She wore a hopeful smile, yet concern crinkled her forehead.

An older woman came pedaling up the drive on a bicycle with a wire basket on the front. Dressed in fitted tan slacks, a black blazer, knee-high black boots, and a black helmet, she looked like she should be riding a horse in a polo match rather than pedaling a bike.

Fanny's good nature vanished, and she glared at the approaching woman. Another one of George's admirers?

The woman's stern gaze narrowed on Declan and me. She slipped her rigid body off the bicycle seat, removed her helmet, and foofed her short gray hair.

Fanny pursed her lips. "What are you doing here? You're certainly not allowed in the house without

George home. Thought you'd sneak in while he's gone, did you?"

"Suddenly you're the estate's caretaker, Fanny? I think not. You wish you were caring for George. No matter how hard you try, this will never be your home. Not with George lying ill in that hospital bed."

Fanny and I gasped at the woman's callous remark.

Declan's gaze darkened. "One of George's cousins, are ya?"

"His cousin Enid," Fanny spat.

"I'm more than capable of introducing myself, thank you." Her gray-eyed gaze narrowed on Declan. "You sound Irish."

When he didn't respond, her gaze narrowed further. "And your names would be?"

"None of your business," Declan said. "I'm sure you're also more than capable of excusing yourself." He gestured to her bike.

"Humph." Nose in the air, Enid turned to her bike to find Mac peeing on the back tire. She swatted a hand at him. "Get away from that, you horrible creature."

"Don't you dare touch him," I said. "He's the new guard dog." I gave Mac a pat on the head.

"Oh my yes, he looks quite intimidating in his little skirt. Well, I'll certainly have the last laugh. You can count on that. I've found an investor who's interested in turning the estate into solicitor offices. Edwards and Price."

Fanny slapped a white-gloved hand on her hip. "You wouldn't dare."

Enid let out a pleased laugh, slipping on her helmet. "Why wouldn't I? George informed us about selling the estate when it's not even on the market. They'll make a deal he won't be able to refuse. If it's even up to him. It will likely be up to the bank." She pedaled away furiously on her bicycle, making the Wicked Witch of the West look like a Welcome Wagon Lady.

Fanny's petite frame went rigid, and her hands balled into fists at her side. "Slag," she muttered.

I wasn't up on British slang, but by the surprised look on Declan's face, it was pretty bad. At least for Fanny.

"George will be devastated if Edwards and Price buys his home. His wife, Diana, ran off with Jonathon Edwards, one of the partners."

My mouth dropped. "Maybe she's lying to upset George."

"Oh, she's serious. That would be exactly something Enid and her cousin Walter in Scotland would do. They aren't worried one bit about the home staying in the family. They're just greedy. If pneumonia doesn't kill George, this will." Tears filled Fanny's eyes, and she cupped a hand over her mouth, capturing a sob.

I slipped an arm around the woman's narrow shoulders. "He's going to be fine."

"They knew George needed money, maybe not precisely how much, but they could have helped him. Of course, the man is too proud to ask family, but they should have offered it if they thought they had any right to the home. They should have been paying their fair share all along. George never told them that Diana ran off with his money, not merely the family solicitor. He was embarrassed enough by the whole scandal. If Enid learns you're related, she'll assume he's leaving you the estate rather than selling it, merely to spite them. Who knows what they'll do."

I couldn't afford to maintain *myself* let alone an English estate. I'd definitely donate it to the National Trust if they'd take it. Or maybe sell it for enough to pay my bills. Ugh. How could I even think such a thing with George lying in the hospital? I sounded like Cousin Enid.

"Nobody is aware of your relationship outside of Thomas and me. Best to keep it that way."

And the nurses in Lancaster. Luckily, the hospital was in a city with high patient traffic and not a small town.

"George should be offering tours of the home and gardens," Fanny said. "He shouldn't lose the estate because his mother became a paranoid recluse, mad as a hatter. He claims he's honoring her wishes by keeping the house closed up, but circumstances have changed, and he's too stubborn to see that. More than a thousand English country homes have been demolished in the past hundred years. It'd be a shame if George's became one of them." She took a calming breath, looking emotionally drained from her rant and our encounter with Enid. Then her eyes widened with shock. "Oh my."

We followed her gaze to a sheep trotting up the drive, making a beeline for the dog-shaped shrubs.

"Enid must have let it in," I said.

Mac took off, yanking his leash from my hand. Barking, he raced toward the sheep, which had at least three hundred pounds on him.

"Mac, stop!" I yelled.

He kept running.

The minute we got home, he was off to obedience school.

Declan set down the wicker basket, and we flew after him. The sheep spotted Mac and slowed its trot. Its head swiveled from the dog to the shrubs back to the dog. They were at a standoff. Mac let out a ferocious bark and ran past the sheep. The sheep decided Mac looked like more fun than the shrubs and chased after him. They ran circles around the sprawling lawn before Mac took off toward the gate, the sheep following. They disappeared around the corner.

"What if Mac runs out the gate and gets hit by a car?" I yelled frantically, chasing after him.

Declan ran ahead and reached the entrance before me. Mac was at the gate, jumping up and down, barking victoriously at his opponent now out on the road. Declan quickly closed the gate.

"I'm going to"—I fought to catch my breath—"kill that slag."

"Look on the bright side. Maybe Mac found his calling. A sheep-herding dog."

I loved the idea of having a field of sheep in rural Ireland by Declan's parents. And Mac having a sense of purpose at such a young age might teach him discipline. It'd taken me twenty-four years to discover my purpose in life and have a sense of direction.

No way was *either* of us leaving Ireland.

Halfway down the drive, we met Fanny speed walking and out of breath. Mac raced toward the house, on an adrenaline high from his successful chase.

"Would you like to come inside for some tea?" I

asked her. One thing I'd learned in Ireland—a spot of tea could remedy anything.

She smiled faintly. "Thank you, dear, but I best be going. I have more baking to do. Tell George I will call on him tomorrow." She appeared to be holding out hope that'd he'd be awake. Her smile faded, and her porcelain cheeks reddened. "We can't let that horrible Enid win. We just can't."

Thomas came running up from the back garden. "Bloody beast didn't get at my shrubs, did it?"

I shook my head.

"I'm going to wrap a chain around that gate until I can get a locksmith out on Monday."

"Enid let it in," Fanny said.

"The slag." Thomas shook his fist at the gate. "When George's mum passed, he stopped locking it. There wasn't enough staff to let in the delivery persons, and he despised the intercom system. The surveillance cameras haven't worked in years. We can no longer afford such an elaborate security system. No need for it now anyhow."

A glint of inspiration shone in Declan's blue eyes. "If George knew about Enid's plans, he'd be wanting to do everything in his power to keep the estate. He'd be all for the art-mystery dinner. It's a bril idea."

I agreed. I'd only known Cousin Enid five minutes and wanted her defeated as much as I wanted George to win! I told Thomas about the woman's plans to turn the estate into law offices associated with George's wife's lover, and our plans to save it. Next to George, Thomas would be most impacted by the sale of the house, despite what Enid thought. Thomas's family had lived here for three generations. And next to Thomas, Fanny would have the most to lose if George was no longer within walking distance from her home.

"George will be furious if she sells it to those crooked thieves," Thomas said. "As if he hasn't been through enough. There's no reason for privacy at this point."

"No reason at all." Fanny's eyes filled with determination. "George will surely change his mind once he learns of his cousin's underhanded plan. We must do whatever it takes to save the estate."

If both Thomas and Fanny were on board, we had to do it.

"Please keep me informed on your plans," Fanny said. "I will help in any way I can." She marched off, gravel crunching under her heels. A woman on a mission.

Being proactive was much better than us doing nothing while we waited around impatiently for George to get well. We could make a nice dent in his bills and have the estate on the road to recovery when he returned home.

"We'll put together a plan and see if we can make it work," I said. "We went to the library to look for old newspaper articles about the theft, but it's closed. Do you remember much about it?"

"That I do," Thomas said. "I was here when it occurred. But I can do better than an old man's failing memory. I'll collect a few items and meet you in the house." He rushed off.

A nervous feeling tossed my tummy. I was due back to work on Monday. I was still in a probationary period earning the CEO's trust and proving myself. I had online classes to take and meetings to plan. Yet how could I ditch George when I'd worked so hard to uncover Grandma's past and connect with her relatives? I'd only known him a month, yet cared more about him than the cousins he'd known his entire life. Grandma had left because she'd obviously felt it was the best choice for them or that she hadn't had a choice. I had a choice. No way was I leaving George without at least trying to help him.

He had nobody else to turn to.

I peered over at the mansion, channeling Mary Crawley from *Downton Abbey*. When working as an on-site meeting staff, I used to always ask myself what Rachel would do in a situation. Now, I asked myself what the strong-willed, confident character Mary would do.

She'd kick Enid's ass across the English Channel for even trying to take Downton from her family.

Cousin Enid was going down!

CHAPTER EIGHT

We unpacked the groceries—tuna salad with corn, egg salad, chicken salad, deli meat... All cold food. Declan and I agreed the massive cast-iron stove was beyond intimidating and our cooking capabilities. We were trying to save George's house, not burn it to the ground.

The small convenience store hadn't sold Tayto chips, so I'd had to settle for an unfamiliar brand. I'd grabbed salt-and-vinegar-flavored crisps by mistake rather than cheese and onion. I took a bite of a chip, and the tangy burst of vinegar made my top lip curl back. I tossed the bag in the garbage. No matter how much I wanted to adapt to the Irish lifestyle, I would never acquire a taste for vinegar and give up ketchup.

I peeked inside the tub of Rachel's favorite flavored ice cream—caramel sea salt vanilla—relieved it hadn't melted. I'd also bought her a stash of energy drinks before I even knew I was going to have to be a total suck-up.

"Getting Rachel on board with the art-mystery

dinner will be more difficult than getting George on board. At least I hope so. George will certainly agree with our idea after he hears Enid's threat."

"She wasn't on board about ya going for the Flanagan's job, but that didn't stop ya, did it now?"

"I'll need her expertise. This is way beyond my Meeting Planning 101 class. I have no clue how to estimate catering guarantees or create a budget when people have to buy into the event. I don't even know how to do a budget for corporate events when the company foots the entire bill. How will we know what to charge? Where will we get money for deposits on tables, chairs...and dishes?"

"I have money from selling my house."

"I can't let you front the money for this. If we don't make a profit, I'll feel horrible."

Even more pressure for the event to succeed. But that was totally sweet that Declan made the offer.

"Made more on the sale than I'd expected. And my donation can be a tax write-off for the restoration of a historical property."

"Could you do that?"

He shrugged. "Why not?"

"What if I don't have time to plan the event? Rachel handed off two Flanagan meetings, both in a few weeks. I have to plan that stupid glamping trip and an incentive to either Vienna, Florence, or Dubrovnik. Not to mention finding Gracie and Bernice's Scottish ancestors, Gretchen's German one, and my grandma's birth record." And I was dying to contact that Scottish couple to see if I could find a family connection with our Coffeys.

Gazing into my eyes, Declan placed his hands on my shoulders and massaged them.

I relaxed slightly.

"You'll have time. I can help you with Florence and Dubrovnik. Work from here. Rachel planned Flanagan's meetings from four thousand miles away."

True. I'd also be planning them from Milwaukee if I had to return there until my citizenship was straightened out. Yet I needed to be visible in the office prior to being deported, or who knew what underhanded tactics Gemma would use to sabotage my job. And if I was four thousand miles away, I'd have to rely on her to ship me massive program binders. She'd likely have the five-hundred-dollar shipping cost taken out of my paycheck.

"I can hear Rachel now. How are you going to juggle the event with your job? How are you going to make enough profit to save this place?"

"So we'll figure out answers to all of her questions before she arrives tonight."

Tick tock...

"I only have a three-day meeting next week in Dublin," Declan said. "I can help out. I'll be the eccentric artist in a silk robe and ascot." He squared his shoulders and put on airs. "All the world's a stage, and all the men and women merely players. They have their exits and their entrances, and one man in his time plays many parts." He arched a brow, wearing a crooked smile. "As shall we."

I clapped. "Wow, I'm impressed. It's not only Oscar Wilde you can quote."

"I had to recite it for a school project. Hadn't a bloody clue what the feck I was saying."

I laughed.

"You can be researching the theft and writing the script as that's your expertise, genealogist supersleuth."

I was feeling more like the bumbling Inspector Clouseau than the highly skilled Sherlock Holmes when it came to genealogy research.

I scrambled for ideas. "It can't be just one dinner. We need to make a ton of money. The festival lasts three days. We could do a mystery dinner each night, and during the day we could offer other events...like painting a stolen masterpiece. Back home wine and painting parties are all the rage with bachelorette parties and groups of girlfriends."

Declan's gaze narrowed. "In Ireland?"

"No, in Milwaukee. Not sure about Ireland."

"Ah, right, then, I thought you said back *home*, which is now Ireland." His lips curled into a smile.

I nodded. "You're right. The power of positive thinking. I can't be putting any negativity into the universe."

"Those painting parties sound grand. We could offer them late afternoon before dinner."

"During the day, we could do something geared toward families. Maybe a scavenger hunt to find the stolen artwork."

"We're going to be wrecked."

My previous on-site job executing meetings had entailed fifteen-hour days. If I was still working long hours, at least it was on my own terms and included things I was passionate about, like this event and genealogy research.

Thomas walked through the back door, carrying two

large scrapbooks. "Everything you need to know about the theft. More than the police even knew."

We headed into the library and sat on the couch with Thomas in the middle. Mac followed but decided to continue on to the salon rather than curling up by the roaring fire. He was taking advantage of the wide-open space before he was cooped back up in our tiny studio apartment.

"I kept a scrapbook on everything that was printed on the theft, hoping to solve it. I never told the family. They wanted no reminders of that evening. It was never to be discussed."

Newspaper articles, handwritten notes, and photographs of the stolen artwork filled the top scrapbook. The worn cover and pages reflected how determined Thomas had been to solve the crime. He opened the cover, and big bold letters read TEN MILLION POUNDS IN PAINTINGS STOLEN! The yellowed newspaper clipping had a picture of George with his hand partially obstructing his face. How mortifying for him.

Thomas took an encouraging breath. "I recall the evening like it was yesterday."

"It must have been terrifying." I slipped my phone from my jeans pocket. "Is it okay if I record this?"

He nodded faintly, dropping back against the couch, staring into the crackling fire he'd made while we were shopping. "It was half eight in the evening. Dinner had just finished, and the family had retired to the library. The kitchen staff had left, and I was putting the finishing touches on a floral arrangement in the foyer. Ivory roses with pink peonies and purple dahlias. Quite lovely." A faint smile curled his lips, then faded.

"The doorbell rang. George answered it. Four men with guns, wearing Beatles masks—the singing group, not the insect—forced their way into the house. The alarm system hadn't been set as the family hadn't turned in for the evening. Ringo demanded we go into the loo, in what was a very poor attempt at a British accent. I'm quite sure they were American. He pointed a gun in the direction of the loo as if he knew precisely where it was located. Diana went hysterical, and the man turned the gun on her. She went pale, and I feared she was going to pass out. It was the one time I actually felt a bit of sympathy for the woman.

"She managed to calm down a bit, and they shut us in the loo, warning us to remain fifteen minutes before coming out. Diana and Isabella refused to come out of the room until the police arrived. When we returned to the salon, eight paintings and a sculpture were missing. They knew precisely what they were doing, taking the most valuable pieces."

Thomas eased out a shaky breath before continuing. "George's mother went to stay with her sister in Scotland for a month. Diana lived with her parents for several months. Even after the installation of an upgraded security system, with panic buttons in each room, Diana didn't return for some time. She wanted to move, but George refused. George's mother spent more and more time with her sister in Scotland. The theft caused a rift in both marriages, tore the family apart." He frowned, an overwhelming sense of despair deepening the wrinkles on his weathered face.

Was that when George's parents started sleeping in separate bedrooms?

"I didn't blame either woman for not returning right away. We jumped at the slightest noise and weren't allowed to answer the door. George's mother was convinced it was an inside job because the thieves knew the location of the loo. George's father fired all the staff except for the cook and me."

"Did you think it was an inside job?" Declan asked.

Thomas shook his head. "Hundreds of people have visited the house over the years and used the loo, and several plumbers had fixed the pipes. We still keep the front door locked to this day and don't open it without good reason. Having been so distraught yesterday upon returning from the hospital, I left it unlocked. I'm glad I did. I wouldn't have opened it, assuming it was unwanted guests." He smiled faintly. "The family was never the same after that."

"I imagine not," I said.

Apparently, Thomas was never the same either. I placed a comforting hand over his trembling one. George would surely have a similar or even worse reaction to reliving that night through the art-mystery event when he hadn't even been allowed to discuss it for over twenty years. And it was the cause of his mother going mad.

"Maybe this event wouldn't be good for George's health. He might find reliving that evening too upsetting."

"No, we'll manage. We'll get through it together. I am even more convinced now that it's the right thing to do. Allowing people in the home will provide George the closure he needs. Help him recover." He nodded. "Yes, it's definitely the right thing to do. If George doesn't have the estate to return to, I fear he won't be leaving the hospital."

I'd had the same fear.

We needed to give George the will to live.

Mac came trotting into the room, carrying something brown in his mouth.

"Did you get into the brown bread on the counter?"

As he approached, the object in his mouth moved.

"Omigod!" I leapt from the couch. "It's a mouse!"

My loud squeal scared the bejeezus out of Mac, and he took off in the other direction. We all flew after him, into the salon. Luckily, he zipped past the stairs rather than racing up them. He peered over his shoulder at us.

"Mac, honey, give that to Mommy." I tried to sound calm while I was freaking out over what kind of disease wild mice might carry. "Do mice have rabies?"

"Don't believe so, but the pesky critters carry a host of other diseases," Thomas said. "I hope he doesn't swallow it."

Swallow it!

We went at Mac from different directions, finally cornering him. His gaze darted between us. Unable to come up with an exit strategy, he dropped the mouse. The poor little creature scurried off and slipped under the door to a room we hadn't yet explored.

I let out a huge sigh, almost collapsing with relief.

"Will have to set the traps again," Thomas said.

As much as I didn't want Mac or any of us getting bitten by a diseased mouse, or to have one scurry across my face while sleeping, or across the salon during our mystery dinner, I couldn't kill one. I'd been devastated upon finding my pet hamster, Bruno, dead on the wheel in his cage. Dad had buried him in the backyard, now next to our cat Izzy.

"Can't you trap it and set it free?" I said.

Thomas looked like he'd never heard of such a thing. "There's certainly more than one."

I gave Declan a pleading look.

"Suppose we could go to a hardware store and see what we can be finding."

Every time I thought it was impossible to love this man any more, he did something to prove I could.

I smiled. "Probably best not to mention it to Rachel. She's scared to death of mice. She used to call my pet hamster a rodent. He once got loose in the house, and she wanted to let our cat Izzy catch him." Mac wasn't even allowed to catch flies.

Was I becoming a bit overbearing like my mother?

CHAPTER NINE

That evening, Declan and I were relaxing on the couch in the library in front of a crackling fire, yet I shivered, unable to get rid of the chill in my body. Even at minus twenty in Wisconsin, I wasn't this cold. The dampness here, especially inside, was a different kind of cold. Once it took hold, you felt it deep down in your bones. I was going to end up sick in the hospital like George.

"I'm going to grab another sweater."

"Here." Declan handed me his blue wool sweater draped over the arm of the couch. He continued paging through the estate's artwork portfolio Thomas had given him as if me wearing his sweater was no big deal.

It wasn't like we were back in the 1950s and Declan was giving me his letterman sweater to wear so everyone knew we were dating. But it was the first time I'd ever worn Declan's clothing. I slipped the blue fisherman's sweater on over my cream one. It felt soft...and intimate and smelled like Declan's woodsy cologne. I snuggled up next to Declan and continued paging through the scrapbook on the theft.

Declan took a sip of whiskey from a crystal glass. "George might have had to sell off most of his belongings, but his taste in whiskey couldn't be bought. This is brilliant."

My gold-colored beverage was tea. I'd found several bottles of red wine in the kitchen cabinet but was afraid they might be pricey. Unfortunately, the tea wasn't doing much to warm me up.

"Why couldn't the stolen paintings have been landscapes?" Declan pointed at a photo with a portrait of a woman. "Vermeer, Goya, Rubens... An impressive collection but a bit more difficult to copy than an Impressionist landscape."

"Your drawing of me is awesome. You'll do a fantastic job."

A text dinged on my phone. It was Zoe inquiring on George's health and attaching pics from St. Patrick's Day at Carter's pub up the road. Her parents were decked out in green, drinking pints with the pub's owner, Des, dressed as St. Patrick, and his wife, Mags, dressed in a green robe-like dress with a white shawl draped across her head and wrapped around her shoulders. Their son Darragh was dressed like a green vampire. I assumed his costume was in memory of the Irish author Bram Stoker. I smiled, wishing we could have joined them for the holiday. The pub's Christmas party had been a blast.

"Who is Mags supposed to be?" I asked.

"St. Brigid of Kildare. A female patron saint."

The doorbell rang.

Mac let out a bark and jumped up from the blanket in front of the fire. He trotted out to the salon.

I froze, my heart hammering. Not for fear it might be thieves preparing to force their way into the house, but because it was Mom and Rachel. Now I knew how the Dalys had felt every time the doorbell rang after the theft.

Declan let out a shaky breath. "Right, then. We should probably be answering that."

I couldn't believe how nervous he was about meeting Mom. She would love Declan after that bastard Andy, even if Rachel still claimed that he was a womanizer and going to hurt me. I was more nervous about selling Rachel on the mystery dinner.

I placed the scrapbook on the cocktail table and slowly stood. "I should explain George's circumstances before they walk into an empty house."

We headed across the foyer. A wave of heat rushed over me as we passed by the fireplace, and then it was gone, rising to the second floor. Hopefully, we'd be toasty warm in bed. We joined Mac, barking at the entrance, anxious to greet our visitors. I opened the door, and he shot out. He jumped up on Rachel, knocking her down a step, and Mom instinctively took a step back in case she was next. It made room for Declan and me on the stoop. I closed the door behind us.

Despite Mom's wrinkled blue knit pantsuit and curly brown hair gone flat, her blue eyes sparkled and she wore a bright smile.

I wrapped her in a hug. "Welcome."

Mac was still jumping on Rachel.

"Stop that," I scolded him.

He ignored me.

Mom clapped her hands. "Mac, get down."

He obediently sat his butt on the step.

I shot him a peeved look for not obeying me in front of company.

"Aren't you festive in your little tutu?" Mom scratched behind Mac's ears, and he wriggled with excitement.

Rachel didn't bother brushing the tan fur from her black yoga pants and jersey cardigan. She gave Declan and me a hug. I introduced Mom and Declan. He held out his hand, but she drew him in for a hug instead.

"It's wonderful to finally meet you," she said.

"Pleased to meet you, Mrs. Shaw."

"Oh goodness, no need to be so formal. Please call me by my first name."

Declan shot me a panicked looked.

I'd never mentioned her first name.

"It's Barbara," Mom said.

Declan flushed with embarrassment. "Sorry 'bout that."

I'd never seen Declan look flustered.

"My fault," I said. "You're Mom to me. Guess I never mentioned your name."

"She downed all the energy drinks I bought at the airport before we were even over New York." Rachel forced a smile, undoubtedly ready for a quiet and comfy bedroom.

I hoped she wouldn't mind that *we* were roomies.

"We needed to stay awake in case of a water landing. I can't believe they allow people to sleep in the exit row. How are they willing and able to assist when they're drugged up on sleeping meds?"

This was Mom's second time flying over water. She and Dad had flown to Hawaii. She'd originally used her fear of flying over a large body of water as an excuse for not visiting Sadie Collentine rather than bitterness toward her mother.

"She even asked a flight attendant if we shouldn't switch seats with two passengers sleeping. Now you're going to have to take sleeping meds to counteract those drinks."

"I can't wait to take a long, hot shower and brush my teeth." Mom rubbed a finger over her teeth.

I wondered if there'd be hot water and enough bath towels for everyone. I hadn't thought to check.

"And it's freezing out here." Rachel tightened the ponytail holding back her brown shoulder-length hair. "Let's get inside."

"Well, it's not a lot warmer in there…" As I explained George's financial situation and lack of furnishings and heat, Mom's expression went from shocked disbelief to concern.

She frowned. "Well, it appears George was like our mother, keeping secrets from family." She heaved a tired sigh as if my information had exhausted her more than sleeping meds would. "Yet this isn't the time to be upset, with George sick in the hospital. After all, he is my brother, and family."

The same forgiving attitude she'd had toward Grandma after my Ireland visit at Christmas when I'd learned about Grandma's first husband, Michael, and them being estranged from their families. However, her attitude had changed when she'd learned about her mother abandoning George as a baby, leaving him with his Daly cousins. She insisted no matter what the circumstances, she'd never have left Rachel or me with relatives. Mom was now more bitter toward her mother than before. I feared she wouldn't forgive her about George if they didn't have the chance to meet.

This was why I dreaded telling Nigel that his great-grandpa had left England as a convict, never to return. The downside of genealogy research was finding skeletons in families' closets that people might be best off not knowing about. Not that I considered George a skeleton in our closet, but Nigel would likely consider his convict ancestor one.

Sometimes ancestry research was a double-edged sword.

Declan opened the door and ushered us inside, following behind with the luggage. The suitcase wheels bounced against the wood floor, echoing through the salon but failing to drown out Mom's and Rachel's gasps. Mom peered up at the crystal chandelier with half the bulbs burned out. Rachel shivered, gravitating toward the fireplace.

"I can't imagine my mother living in such extravagance. Even without furnishings, it's quite impressive. To have had meals cooked for you and your house cleaned. To think George grew up here, while Dottie and I shared a bedroom and five of us shared one bathroom."

I wouldn't mention that his mother had been mad as a hatter. Maybe she hadn't been during his childhood. If Mom thought Grandma had left her son with an unfit mother, she'd be even more upset with her.

Mom's gaze narrowed on the cobwebs linking the

staircase spindles. "Did George also sell his cleaning supplies? I'll make sure the house is spick and span before he comes home from the hospital."

We all smiled, nodding as if we were confident about George's recovery.

"The place reminds me of that estate in Brussels, where we did the off-site dinner," Declan told Rachel, attempting to nonchalantly segue into a conversation about the mystery event.

Rachel nodded faintly. "That was a gorgeous place. The rental alone was half our budget. Brecker had just bought a Belgium beer company."

"Wouldn't this be an awesome venue for an event?" I said. "And no rental fee. We'd just have to pay for catering and..."

Rachel's gaze narrowed. "Are you thinking Brecker or Flanagan's should hold an event here?"

I shook my head. "Us." I gestured to everyone.

"Why would *we* hold an event here?" she asked.

"To save the estate." I excitedly described Declan's and my ideas for the art-mystery event.

Rachel let out a faint laugh. "Are you serious?"

I squared my shoulders, maintaining a confident and determined attitude despite my worries over pulling it off. "Totally. We could do it."

"Remember that event you planned in Tuscany in only two weeks after the other villa closed?" Declan said.

Rachel bit down on her lower lip, undoubtedly counting to ten, trying not to lose her patience. "Where would we get money for the deposits?"

"I just sold my house."

"Oh, congratulations," Mom said. "Are you going to buy another place or rent your own apartment?"

Own apartment. Very subtle. I gave her a warning look, but her curious, and seemingly innocent, gaze was focused on poor Declan.

He brushed off her meddling comment with a charming smile. "Ah, haven't quite decided yet."

"Caity was so lucky to get a small studio. The perfect size for living alone."

Mortified, I opened my mouth to respond, but Rachel spoke up.

"How did we go from discussing the event to apartment rentals?" She peered over at me. "An event like that would cost a ton when you don't even have furniture. You'd be lucky to break even, let alone make a profit. You have a full-time job now. And I just handed those meetings off to you."

"That's all I'm working on besides an executive glamping trip." And a European incentive I wouldn't mention. She'd freak out that I wasn't qualified to plan it. Like I was freaking out.

Rachel's nose scrunched. "Glamping trip?"

"I'll tell you about it later."

"What does Matthew McHugh think about you working from England after just starting?"

I shrugged. "You planned Flanagan's meetings from four thousand miles away. It doesn't matter where I'm at."

"You haven't told him you're here, have you? What if he asks you to come into the office Monday? You going to hop a plane back to Dublin?"

"The office is near the airport."

Rachel rolled her eyes.

"I'm going to tell him."

She'd really freak if she knew about my challenge obtaining Irish citizenship.

"I can't leave George while he's in the hospital, and we don't know if he's going to make it. I'm the reason we're here. We're his only family besides his aunt Emily, who's in the Canary Islands and hasn't even checked up on him, and Sadie and Seamus, who won't leave Ireland to visit." I'd wait until morning to fill them in on nasty Cousin Enid. "George connected with us because of me." My voice trembled. My bottom lip quivered.

Rachel's gaze softened. "That doesn't make you responsible for saving his home."

"Who else is going to help him?"

Mom placed a hand gently on my arm. "It's so sweet you want to help him, dear, but that would be an awfully big endeavor in such a short period of time. We'll make sure George finds a nice home. No furnishings will certainly make moving much easier." She stifled a yawn. "This discussion can wait until morning when we aren't all so tired. I need a shower and a soft bed."

Rachel and I were just smoothing things over after I went for the Flanagan's position without her blessing. I needed to tread lightly. Seeing George in the hospital tomorrow better get her on board. With or without her help, I was planning the event.

I noticed movement out of the corner of my eye. My gaze darted over to the mouse's brown head peeking out from under the door behind Rachel and Mom. I gasped in surprise.

Having seen it too, Declan said, "How about I be showing ya to your rooms?" He lifted the suitcases, heading toward the stairs before Rachel or Mom could ask about my reaction.

"Sounds like a great idea," Mom said.

We'd left the bedroom doors open to warm up the rooms. From the pink walls and frilly bedding and pillows, I assumed Rachel's room had been George's mom's. I showed Mom to ours, no longer wanting to be my sister's roomie and spend a sleepless night arguing with her.

Mom eyed the silver pail in the corner without commenting, then peered over at the bed. "Such a lovely frame."

The blue quilt was turned down on the four-poster bed, and blue folded bath towels lay on the end. Luckily, each room had its own bath. Flames jumped around in the fireplace. *Thank you, Declan.*

She swept a hand over the back of the rocking chair. Was she envisioning her mother rocking George to sleep like I had?

"You've always taken care of the family," I said. "And Rachel has always looked out for me. I've only had myself to watch out for, and I haven't done the best job at it. I want to be the one to take care of the family for once."

Mom gave me a sympathetic smile. "You've done that by finding George."

I helped Mom hoist her suitcase up on a worn cream upholstered bench at the foot of the bed.

"And now he needs us."

"I understand, dear. And we'll be here to support

and take care of him. But you have enough to worry about with your new job and move to Ireland. Don't overwhelm yourself."

It irked me that she still worried about my ability to take care of myself, let alone others.

She slipped her red velour robe from her suitcase. Its purple zipper was the third replacement zipper, and a pink patch covered a hole on one elbow. I'd offered to buy her a new robe for Christmas two years in a row, but she was attached to the garment she'd probably worn home from the hospital after I was born. Too bad I hadn't brought my white plush robe from La Haute Bohème, a hotel in Prague. Yet it would have taken up my entire brown carry-on bag. I'd already only packed enough clothes for two days, having planned on leaving tomorrow.

"We'll discuss it tomorrow," she said. "Okay?"

While I was growing up, Mom would always say, "We'll discuss it tomorrow," hoping by the next day I'd forget about whatever it was she hadn't wanted to discuss. I never did.

Mac hopped up on the bed and rolled around.

"Ah, sorry, no room for bed hogs. You'll be sleeping with Daddy tonight."

Daddy? I slid Mom a sideways glance to catch her reaction, but her back was to me.

"I'm not sure if it's a good time to mention this." She turned toward me, distressed lines creasing her forehead. "But Andrew called for you right before I left."

A sick feeling tossed my stomach. But nothing compared to the sheer panic that used to press so hard against my chest I feared my lungs would collapse.

Certain situations, smells, or the mere mention of his name no longer triggered such a volatile reaction. However, his demeaning comments still occasionally made me doubt myself.

"What did he want?" I asked cautiously.

"For you to call him. That's all he'd say. He wants to discuss something with you."

That I was part of his twelve-step program and he finally realized he was a narcissistic, controlling ass? Yeah, right. So why had he called? Was he going to once again demand I give him *my* painting, which he claimed was *his*? I had no desire to call him back, but if I didn't, would he start stalking me again? Yet he might start stalking again if I did!

"Declan seems like a great catch. Quite handsome, and that accent..."

"Yeah, so don't scare him away. No more drilling him about his living situation." Yet I was kind of wondering about it myself seeing as it didn't sound like Declan had started apartment hunting.

"What? I merely asked his plans because he'd sold his house. I know you wouldn't jump into living together before you really get to know him."

I did a mental eye roll, taking my green *Coffey Dublin* T-shirt and plaid leggings over by the fire to change. "I'm tired. Let's talk about it tomorrow."

Two could play at that.

CHAPTER TEN

My eyes shot open. I squinted back the sun shining through the windows. Mom used to wake me up for school by throwing up the shades and pulling off my blankets. I wasn't a morning person, unlike Rachel who'd be dressed and studying at the kitchen table when I dragged my butt down for a bowl of cereal. But it wasn't the sun that had woken me. It was shouting from the salon downstairs.

It was 8:00 a.m. Who had the energy to fight at this early hour? I'd barely slept, thanks to Mom's restless legs syndrome. It was like she was racing through Walmart, snatching up deals on Black Friday. And Bernice and Gracie's ancestor James McKinney had run through my mind. What was I missing that I couldn't locate his or his siblings birth records in Scotland? Maybe I should have let Mac sleep with us. He was a total bed hog, and I might have ended up sleeping better on the cold wooden floor.

Omigod. Mac hadn't caught the mouse again, had he? And that was Rachel hollering downstairs?

I hopped out of bed and raced stocking-footed across the room in my jammies, wrapped in my long red coat and blue mohair scarf. The fire had gone out during the night, and it had seemed easier, and safer, to throw on more clothes than to blindly build my first fire in the dark. I flew into the hallway and peered over the railing at Cousin Enid dressed in green riding attire, shaking a fist at Mom, who was threatening to blast her with furniture spray. I'd rather the mouse had returned than that wretched woman. Thomas was grasping the handles of his hedge clippers. Rachel, about the same height as our short uncle, tightened the sash on George's navy velour robe. Declan and Mac had just returned from a walk. Mac ran over and growled at Enid.

I ran down the stairs.

Mom's gaze darted to me. "She said she's George's cousin, so I figured it was okay to let her in."

"And I'm not leaving until you tell me what you've done with all the bloody paintings and furnishings," Enid roared. "You had no right to sell—"

"George had to pay for new plumbing, insurance, roof repairs..." Thomas sliced his hedge clippers in frustration, and Enid snapped her head back.

I needed to check the silver bucket in the bedroom to make sure it hadn't rained last night and the ceiling hadn't leaked.

"It takes money to keep this place running, and you and your cousin Walter never offered to help."

"How dare George sell our family's heritage without even consulting me. That Victorian settee was my grandmother's." She gestured to an empty corner by the fireplace. "It was supposed to be mine." Enid sucked in a shaky breath. Her body trembled with anger.

She was seriously upset about the chair. I couldn't believe the nasty woman had a sentimental bone in her body.

"It was his to sell," Thomas said. "Now go. I'm done listening to your nonsense."

"I have more right to be here than any of you."

Mom squared her shoulders. "I have more right than you, being George's sister."

Enid gasped in shock. "Sister?" Her gaze narrowed. "George doesn't have a sister."

Mom had only been here twelve hours, and she'd managed to disclose our identity and George's unfurnished home to Enid. I'd planned to fill Mom and Rachel in on everything this morning but hadn't expected Enid to barge in at the crack of dawn!

"Yes, he does," Mom said.

"What proof do you have?" Enid asked.

What proof *did* we have? George's birth certificate had likely been altered to note his parents as Henry Wood and Isabella Daly, or he'd have discovered his adoption. However, his baptismal record probably noted Grandma and Michael Daly as his real parents. Just what I needed. One more historical document to not be able to find.

"DNA," I blurted out. "We can do an ancestry DNA test to prove they're related." As if I was going to swab George's cheek or obtain his spit while he was lying in the hospital.

Enid gave her eyes an exaggerated roll. "You could

rig a test. How precisely do you *claim* to be related?" Her thin lips curled into a devious smile. "Isabella had an affair, did she? So George isn't biologically a Daly and involved in yet another scandal?"

I slapped a hand on my hip rather than across the bitch's face like I wanted to. "Oh no, believe me, he's a Daly."

But what if the DNA test proved George wasn't a *Coffey*? That he wasn't related to us? Nigel's mom had discovered she wasn't a hundred percent English but was also French and German, thanks to a DNA test. Nigel had only pursued his ancestry research because of his mom's test results, and that was why I'd discovered the convict ancestor. I believed George's claim that he was Grandma's son. Why would he have lied? Yet what if his mother had lied? DNA tests now made me nervous.

Enid let out a sadistic laugh that sent a chill racing through me. "We'll see about that. Doesn't matter. The place will soon be sold, and I'll receive a nice finder's fee. I'll also have free legal services so I can sue George for my share of the family's fortune."

I gave Thomas a worried look, which he returned. If she sued, George would have to file bankruptcy or flee England. We might both be forced to leave our ancestors' homeland!

Rachel glared at Enid. "Maybe we should do a true-crime *murder*-mystery dinner rather than one solving the art theft."

Did this mean Rachel was on board or bluffing because Enid had ticked her off?

Panic filled Enid's gray eyes. "What are you talking about?"

"We're holding a fundraiser to help George save the estate," Rachel said. "Guests have the opportunity to solve the theft."

"I should think not," Enid spat.

Declan quirked a curious brow. "Guilty, are ya?"

"Of course not. But we won't have you embarrassing the entire family by bringing up a crime that never would have happened if George's family had taken appropriate measures to prevent it. George will be disgraced if everyone learns he allowed the estate to go to ruins." Her self-confidence wavered as she apparently realized *she'd* also be disgraced. "It'll be over my dead body that event happens."

"Whatever it takes." Rachel got in Enid's face, forcing her to step back, momentarily throwing her off her game.

"You'll be sorry." Nose in the air, Enid spun around and huffed out, her bootheels clomping against the wood floor.

Mom lowered the can of furniture polish, and Thomas relaxed his grip on the hedge clippers.

I filled Mom and Rachel in on Enid's plans for turning the estate into law offices and Diana having run off with a partner.

"Maybe instead of a mystery *dinner*, it could be afternoon tea," Rachel said. "That'd be more cost effective. And if it's tea, we wouldn't have to rent tables and chairs. We could use the old couch in the library, bring the settee down from my room... Perhaps it's the one Enid's looking for."

"Wouldn't that get her goat." Mom shook a fist toward the door.

"I have two couches and some chairs we could use," Thomas said.

"We could make finger sandwiches ourselves," I said. "We wouldn't need to hire a caterer to prepare a hot meal."

Rachel smiled. "Exactly. Cost savings."

Mom sniffed the air. "I should have the place cleaned and the musty smell gone in two weeks."

"We'll be explaining that all the original paintings are in storage, not wanting another to get nicked," Declan said. "So George won't be embarrassed a' tall. The reproductions will be hanging on the wall."

"We'll find furniture and antiques at charity shops," Thomas said. "Only need enough to fill the salon and library."

"I'll start making a list of appetizers." Mom tapped a finger against her lips. "I can make those little wieners in a barbecue sauce."

Rachel and I exchanged worried glances as Mom rattled off our traditional Christmas Eve party food list. Not appropriate food for a proper English tea, but she needed to contribute. However, she'd likely change her mind about the party wienies once she saw the behemoth of a stove. She was the queen of crockpot recipes.

"And Fanny Bing, who fancies George, is a great baker," Declan said.

I nodded. "I know where we can get an eclectic array of teapots and dishes for a steal."

"The art supplies I ordered online will be here tomorrow. I can see what Lancaster has so I can get started today."

A look of determination filled Rachel's eyes. "I have ten days off. I'll take a few more. I'm not losing my vacation time again this year. We need to advertise ASAP. Create a website so people can book tickets. We won't have to buy food until we know the precise number attending, two days prior. We need to start spreading the word."

Cousin Enid might be a slag, but she was a motivating slag!

&

Not wanting to take a chance on Mac misbehaving at the hospital, Declan took him when he left to buy art supplies. Neither of the nurses from the previous day was at the reception desk.

A middle-aged woman in a teal-colored uniform glanced up at us. "What is your relationship to the patient?"

"I'm his sister." Mom's eyes watered. "He's my brother, and I might not..." She choked back a sob. "...get to say hello before I have to say good-bye." A tear trailed down her cheek.

Rachel slipped an arm around Mom's shoulder, and the nurse gave her a tissue and a sympathetic smile. She advised us there was no change in George's condition. The meds were still knocking him out, and the fluid remained on his lungs. Mom blew her nose and wiped away her tears. Rachel escorted her down the hall toward George's room, while I hung back and warned the nurse about a crazy woman named Enid who might stop by and shouldn't be allowed to visit George.

She would upset him even if he *had* been in a coma.

I joined Rachel and Mom outside George's room, where Mom was taking deep, calming breaths, shaking it off. She nodded, and we stepped inside to loud snoring and beeping monitors. George looked even paler, still breathing through an oxygen mask, an IV in his arm. Mom grasped the bed rail, steadying herself.

"He has Grandma's chin," I said. "Her heart-shaped face."

Mom nodded, smiling.

"I told him that when we met in Prague."

She placed a hand on my arm. "I'm glad you mentioned that to him."

I set Fanny's basket of scones on the nightstand. Mom slipped a framed picture of her parents, sisters, and her from her purse and put it next to Fanny's tulips. She then removed a tarnished silver brooch with emerald-colored stones that Grandma had worn when she married Michael Daly. Mom had worn it for her wedding, unaware of her mother's first marriage at the time. Mom massaged a thumb over the heirloom as if trying to buff it.

"You should have this," she told George, placing it on the blanket next to his hand. "Our mother wore it on her wedding day." She sucked in a shaky breath, then eased it out. "I can't believe my mother kept him a secret when we could have gotten to know each other years ago. She should have at least left a note in her will if she didn't want anyone to know while she was alive."

Mom enveloped George's hand in hers. "Even after I wrote that poem in fourth grade, she didn't confess I had a brother." Mom took an encouraging breath. "I want a brother named Barry, not a sister named Teri. One who will beat up Lenny Fritz, who tried to give me a kiss. One who will..." Mom's eyes widened. "He just clutched my hand."

Our gazes darted to their hands. George's moved slightly. A twitch more than a clasp, but it was comforting to think he might be able to hear us.

The door opened and Fanny Bing entered, wearing a blue-and-white floral-patterned dress under her blue coat and a fancy blue hat. "Oh my, I'm sorry. I didn't realize George had company. I'll come back."

"Nonsense," Mom said. "Come in."

I introduced George's friend to Rachel and Mom.

"I'm here earlier than I'd expected. Mary is minding the church bake sale, so I didn't have to wait until this evening."

"About your scones..." I explained how our art-mystery event would now be afternoon tea and asked if she'd provide her yummy baked goods.

Fanny's face lit up. "What a lovely idea. I can also make lemon poppy seed and blueberry ones. And Mary has a cupboard full of homemade jams. The woman is obsessed with making jam. Emma makes wonderful cucumber and salmon sandwiches. We'll start spreading the word at the bake sale today. I'm sure others will want to be involved. Everyone loves George." Fanny's porcelain cheeks flushed a light pink, the color of her lipstick.

Some loved him more than others.

"That'd be great," I said. "We'll reimburse you for all costs, of course."

"You'll do no such thing. George refuses to accept my help, but now he has no choice. We all want to see him keep the estate, except his nasty cousin Enid, of course."

"And if you have any furnishings you'd like to loan us, we need to fill up the salon and the library."

"That would be nice for George to not come home to an empty house. He always comments on how much he likes my blue couch. It was my grandmother's. I had it reupholstered."

I told her about our encounter with Cousin Enid and her threat to prove George wasn't a Daly.

"I would think George was baptized at St. Catherine's, where the bake sale is today. I'll ask Pastor Alldridge if he might have a look at the baptismal register for George's record."

Grandma and Michael had been married Protestant, but I couldn't recall if their marriage record had noted the name of the church.

"That'd be great. Hopefully, we won't need it."

But all the better if it noted Grandma and Michael Daly as his parents.

Fanny peered over at Mom. "Will you be making your mother's delicious brown bread? George had me over for tea one day and told me it was his mother's recipe."

Mom nodded hesitantly. "At least she shared her secret recipe with us, even though she didn't share all her secrets."

"Neither did George's mother. So sad you didn't

have the chance to get to know him sooner." She peered over at George lying in bed. "That this is what brought everyone together. He was so happy to have found your family, never having had any siblings, merely his nasty cousins."

"What were his parents like?" Mom said. "Did he have a happy childhood?"

Please don't mention his mum had been mad as a hatter if she had been before the theft.

Fanny nodded. "They were good people. Didn't put on airs like so many who live in such style. I'd never even heard a rumor of them not being his biological parents."

I'd been surprised Cousin Enid hadn't known the truth. Yet if her parents had been closer to George's family than she had, they'd likely been willing to keep the secret. And the woman was several years younger than George.

"It happened so long ago, I suppose not many were around to spread the rumor, and the family led a quiet life even before the theft. But I'll let George tell you more once he's better."

We all nodded reassuringly that George would be up in no time and reminiscing about his childhood on the Daly Estate.

Fanny gazed over at George, a sentimental look on her face. "George and my husband, Bernard, were best friends growing up. We moved to Scotland many years ago for Bernard's job, but he and George stayed in touch as much as they could. After Bernard passed away, I moved back here. It was so nice to come home. To spend time with George..." Fanny's eyes watered.

"He's going to be just fine." Mom embraced Fanny's petite form.

I walked out before I started bawling and gave Mom and Fanny a moment alone with George. Rachel joined me in the hall.

My sister's gaze darkened. "All these years we had an uncle and never knew. We could have been there for him when that bitch left him with nothing and helped him figure out a way to save the estate so he hadn't had to sell off his heritage."

This was the first time I'd heard Rachel sound bitter toward Grandma.

"We can't judge Grandma when we don't know what she went through." Was I a hypocrite or what? *I'd* been judging Grandma. "We're here now to help."

"One weekend of events isn't going to save the place. We need to look at the big picture, a long-term plan to sustain the estate." Rachel's gaze darted back and forth. A pensive, determined look I'd seen before.

She was right. This event was merely a Band-Aid. But it was a start.

If anyone could come up with a solution, it was Rachel.

However, I was quite proud that I was becoming more proactive, no longer always scrambling to recover *after* a disaster had occurred. At least now I was better able to foresee the disasters. Except for George's circumstances.

I certainly hadn't seen that one coming.

CHAPTER
ELEVEN

When we returned to George's house, a small black car sat in the drive. A tall man with short dark hair, rugged good looks, jeans, and a brown sweater was talking to Declan.

Gerry Coffey.

Rachel's face lit up. She peered in the rearview mirror, smoothing a hand over her ponytail and wiping a spec of mascara from under an eye. "I can't believe he's here." Her gaze darted to me. "Did you know he was coming?"

I shook my head.

"He could help Mom and Fanny with the catering. How perfect would that be? He does group events all the time."

They apparently hadn't discussed the status of them dating other people, or that leprechaun chick at the bar. It bode well for Gerry that he'd hauled his cookies over to England to discuss the matter in person. And that I wasn't the one forced to tell Rachel about the woman.

Fingers crossed my sister kept that in mind when he dropped the bomb.

"Who is that?" Mom asked.

"A friend," Rachel said, hopping out of the car. She ran over and greeted Gerry with a fairly intense kiss.

"Not how I'd normally greet a *friend*," Mom said.

"That's Gerry Coffey, my landlord."

Mom smiled. "Oh, how nice to finally put a face with his voice."

How did she know what Gerry's voice sounded like?

I glared over my shoulder at Mom in the backseat, and her smile faded. "You've been talking to Gerry on the phone, checking up on me?" So much for her confidence in my ability to survive on my own in Dublin. "I can't believe you'd do that."

"I honored your wish to not call you every day, but I had to know that you were all right. I'm your mother. And I'm not going to apologize." She stepped out of the car.

I reined in my anger, reminding myself that we were both stressed to the max right now. I didn't want an argument to send either of us over the edge.

Rachel introduced Mom and Gerry. He acted like it was their first time speaking. Nice try.

"You aren't both leaving me for Irish fellows, are you?"

I doubted Rachel would be.

My sister flushed at Mom's comment.

I nodded hello to Gerry, giving him an encouraging smile.

Good luck. Poor bloke was going to need it.

Mom, Declan, and I headed inside.

"So nice to finally meet your landlord," Mom said. "What a nice man, giving you such a great deal on an apartment that is the perfect size..." *For one?* She trailed off, noticing my look warning her to proceed with caution.

Declan brushed it off, smiling at Mac racing up and down the stairs, chasing his shadow rather than a mouse.

"His energy is exhausting," I said.

Declan walked over to an easel in the middle of the foyer, a sheet of plastic covering the floor under it.

"See you found painting supplies," I said.

He raised a halting hand. "Don't be looking. It's not finished."

"Can't I please just peek?"

He relented, stepping back from the painting.

Mom and I walked over and viewed the work in progress. Lots of dark green with a few swooshes of red and yellow and rudimentary outlines of...something. If this painting didn't turn out, I hoped Declan wouldn't give up on his art.

"That's lovely," Mom said.

I nodded enthusiastically. "Incredible. You really captured the green..."

"You haven't a clue what it is," Declan said.

I studied the canvas, hoping it would take form.

He pointed at several brown brushstrokes. "That's a desk...and a woman..."

"Ah," I said as if the painting suddenly became clear.

"I just started the bloody yoke. You're not seeing any of that."

I about collapsed with relief that it wasn't nearly finished.

"Well, I'm sure it will be magnificent when it's done." Mom peered around at the empty walls. "I can't imagine having such paintings to begin with and then to have them taken from you in such a horrific way."

The front door flew open, and Rachel marched inside, the sound of car tires spitting gravel outside. She slammed the door, and the echo vibrated through the room and my chest. I expected the stained-glass window to shatter. Gerry was apparently free to date all the slutty leprechauns he wanted to.

Rachel plastered on a perky smile. "We better get planning the event. No time to waste."

"Okay," I said. "We could go buy dishes." I didn't want to use Grandma's delicate teacups or any of the Daly china and have guests break what few family heirlooms remained.

Yet china shopping probably wasn't the best idea with Rachel's mood.

"I'll meet you in the car." She marched out with as much fervor as she'd entered, and we all cringed, preparing for the slamming door.

"Guess she doesn't want to talk about it," Mom said. "What a shame when he came all the way from Ireland to see her. I'll stay here and clean, keep Declan company while he paints. We can get to know each other better."

Declan wore an uneasy smile.

I gave Mom a cautious look that said not to drill him about apartment hunting. I'd rather have her share embarrassing childhood stories or pictures of me running naked through the sprinkler when I was two, refusing to wear a swimsuit.

I still hated swimsuit shopping.

❧ ❧

An awkward silence filled the car until Rachel zipped around a sharp corner and I let out a gasp of fear. My white-knuckled grip tightened on the door handle of the compact rental car. A good thing Mac had stayed home or Rachel's car would also smell like he had puked up a fruit stand.

"Can you please slow down?"

"Sorry." She eased up on the accelerator, and my blood pressure lowered slightly.

Had Gerry mentioned that I'd seen him with that other woman? Was she pissed I hadn't told her, even though it hadn't been my place to tell? If Gerry hadn't told her I'd known, I should act clueless about the reason for their fight.

"Are you okay?" I asked.

"Yep, perfect. Better to know now that he's a cheating bastard than to find out later."

"But you guys weren't really dating, you said. You never called and wished him a happy Valentine's Day after he mailed you that card. You e-mailed him a thank-you. Blew it off like it was nothing. What's he supposed to think?"

Rachel's gaze darted to me. "Are you taking his side?"

"No, I'm just saying, in all fairness, you guys weren't

exclusive. The fact that you're upset shows how much you care."

"*Did* care."

I wanted to assure Rachel that when her name had come up at the pub, Gerry hadn't given that chick another look. But if I confessed that I'd known, she might drive off the road in a mad frenzy and take out some innocent sheep in a field.

"I don't want to talk about him, all right?"

"Okay, fine."

I let it go, even though Rachel didn't hesitate to butt her nose into my relationship with Declan. Not to sound selfish, but this better not affect my current living situation above Coffey's pub, not to mention my friendship with Gerry. Outside of Emily Ryan, he was the only person I knew in Dublin.

Finding it odd that Emily still hadn't checked on George, I resent my original e-mail. Maybe the first one had gotten lost in cyberspace.

Ten minutes later, we were browsing among the teacups outside Nicole's Vintage Finds.

"The mismatched ones are half the price and would add a bit of eclectic charm," I said.

Rachel selected a blue floral cup and a yellow saucer. She stared at the delicate china. "How sad to think each lonely piece was once part of a full set that a couple picked out for their wedding or had been passed down to them through generations. And now a cup doesn't even have a matching saucer."

I was usually the sentimental one, not Rachel.

She was a total basket case over Gerry.

"I'm so glad you discovered that Grandma's teacup

collection was from our Flannery family's china company and not a hodgepodge of ones she'd randomly collected over the years." Rachel's voice cracked, and she cleared her throat. "Thank God Aunt Teri is a hoarder and had them stored away in her basement." She sucked in a shaky breath.

Was she going to cry? I honestly didn't know if I'd seen my sister cry in her adult life. I wished she would. That might sound callous, but she could use a good cry. Letting out her emotions, other than an occasional fit of anger over work, would be good for her physically and emotionally. Keeping stress bottled up inside had damaged her kidney. She'd had a major kidney infection in college, and when she got too stressed out, her right kidney throbbed.

"You know he talks about you nonstop?" I said.

"Thanks." Rachel placed a cup and saucer in an empty wooden bin. "But I'm really not ready to talk about it."

I reluctantly let it go. For now.

"How many cups do you think we need?" I asked.

"We have to cram as many people as possible into the library. If we sell fifty tickets at a hundred pounds each, that's five thousand pounds per event."

"I hope we sell fifty tickets period."

"We need to do two back-to-back events daily so we sell three hundred tickets for thirty thousand pounds."

I envied the way Rachel could do math in her head and rattled off numbers like nothing. I was lucky my math was correct when I used a calculator.

"So that's seventy-five pounds for fifty teacups," she said. "And we need a few extras in case of breakage."

"If the events are back to back, we'll need at least two hours between them for washing dishes and resetting."

Dessert plates cost one pound each. Two matched here, three there. Teapots were ten pounds. A deal, but pricey for our budget. Rachel hadn't yet created our budget, but I knew it wasn't much. I wasn't letting Declan pitch in more than the art supplies if he didn't have to.

"People will have to share teapots," she said. "We'll only offer two or three kinds of tea, so fewer pots."

The shop owner joined us and introduced herself as Nicole Duvall. She was American, thirtyish, with bangs and long dark hair, dressed in jeans and a cozy cream sweater.

"Where are you from in the States?" Rachel said.

"Southern Arizona, wine country. Moved here five years ago."

"How'd you manage to get citizenship?" I asked.

"My husband's British. He grew up in this area and was in Arizona for a month on business when we met."

I smiled, yet was disappointed that she couldn't provide some helpful insight into obtaining foreign citizenship.

"Do you happen to sell silverware?" Rachel asked.

She eyed our bins filled with china. "Are you hosting a tea party?"

I explained the event.

Her blue eyes widened. "Well, I'd certainly come. Would love to see the inside of that place."

"Do you have any furniture for sale?" Rachel asked. "Like couches and chairs? We don't have quite enough seating."

She shook her head. "Just a few occasional tables. But if you need couches and chairs, I know where you can get a few for a small donation. I belong to the local theater group. We have some furniture, props, and 1920s attire."

"Did you do a *Downton Abbey* play?" I asked.

"No, we perform a Hercule Poirot play every three months. Are you familiar with the detective series?"

We nodded. Mom watched it on PBS.

"We might need a few actors also," I said.

"I'm in." Nicole smiled. "I can close for lunch and take you to get the costumes." She went over to lock up.

"It'll be just like when we were growing up and you wrote plays to perform in the backyard," Rachel said to me. "I was always inside studying or creating a business plan for my first company."

Rachel's entrepreneurial spirit began with a lemonade stand. Not your typical boring lemonade but flavors such as peach, blackberry, and watermelon. She'd even created a list with suggestions for combining flavors. She'd put Courtney Shepherd's stand out of business in one afternoon.

"I wished I'd have participated," she said. "It always looked like so much fun."

Rachel envied the play productions I'd done in the backyard? I'd never seen her so wistful and melancholy.

Could this day get any weirder?

CHAPTER TWELVE

Upon our return to George's, the sheep were once again blocking the road, munching on shrubs. Rachel laid on the horn, still releasing her anger over Gerry. The animals ignored her. She pressed the horn repeatedly. When they didn't budge, she rolled down the window and screamed at them. Freaked out by the crazy woman behind the wheel, they raced off, vanishing around the corner. I'd have to remember that tactic.

The padlocked chain wrapped around the gate poles gave the illusion it was secured to keep out Enid and the sheep. However, the lock wasn't clamped tightly because Thomas only had one key. I unwrapped the chain and peered around for sheep lurking nearby before opening the gate. Rachel drove in. I put the chain and padlock back in place.

Rachel hauled a bin of teacups and plates inside while I carried the theater's costumes. The crushed velvet and satin fabrics, decorative beads, and sequins weighted down my arms. How had the thin women in *Downton Abbey* worn such heavy dresses?

Declan, Mom, Thomas, and Mac were admiring Declan's finished painting on the wall—a woman seated at a desk writing a letter, sun shining through the window. It was so realistic it helped take away the chill in the room. And the smell would be gone before long. A spare bag of charcoal must have been lying around. Mom had placed charcoal-filled tin pans throughout the room. She claimed it was the best natural dehumidifier and removed musty smells. Not only did we need to freshen up the place for the event, but for George's health so he didn't end up back in the hospital.

Would a tray of charcoal get rid of the stinky smell in Declan's car?

"The painting bears a remarkable resemblance to the original." Thomas shuddered. His chill likely wasn't from the breeze blowing through the open windows, helping the charcoal air out the place. It was from memories of that evening. The same reaction George might experience upon seeing the paintings. "A bit strange having it hang there after twenty years. As if it were recovered and put back in its proper place."

"It's absolutely lovely." Mom placed a hand on Declan's shoulder.

He wore a proud look. "Feels good to be painting again. I'm not as rusty as I'd feared."

"It's awesome." I gave him a kiss, our lips barely touching before he drew back with a nervous smile.

Seriously? Now I couldn't even give him a fleeting kiss in front of my mom? She better not have brought up his housing situation again.

Mom eyed the costumes draped over my arm. "Did you go clothes shopping?"

"No, the theater group in town is letting us borrow them. Unsure what would fit everyone, we brought them all."

Mom held up a long black-beaded burgundy dress. "Oh, my favorite color. I'll take this one."

Rachel and I turned up our noses at a deep-blue flouncy dress with layers of chiffon wrapped around the neckline.

She snagged the next dress—champagne-colored satin with clear beads and matching long satin gloves. She held it up in front of her, and the bottom puddled on the floor. "I'll have to wear some really high heels. I love it."

I chose a jade-colored dress with black embroidery and flowing chiffon sleeves. Very Irish. A headband with green poufy feathers hung around its hanger.

Declan and Thomas checked out the suits.

"Pants all look a bit wide, I'd say. I best be wearing my black suit with this white bowtie and vest." Declan hooked a finger around the garment's hanger.

Thomas chose a brown tweed suit. Exactly how I'd pictured him dressing before we'd met.

We dispersed to our rooms to try on our costumes. The jade dress was a bit big, but Mom assured me she could alter it with pins. I positioned the feathered band on my head. A few bobby pins would help keep it in place. Mom looked elegant in the burgundy dress. The only time I could recall her wearing a dress was occasionally to church.

We congregated back in the library. Rachel's champagne-colored, size two satin dress fit perfectly except for the length. Thomas's tweed suit jacket swallowed his narrow shoulders, but he seemed pleased with it. Declan looked insanely hot in his black suit, white shirt, tie, and vest. Big surprise.

"Reminds me of when you girls used to play dress-up in Mom's church clothes and fancy hats." Mom adjusted her hat—black with a gold brooch attached to a burgundy band. "We really should wear more hats in the States."

It was reassuring that Mom had a precious memory rather than a bitter one toward her mother. She hadn't had any of her grandmother's dresses to wear because she'd never known her.

"Rachel always wore Grandma's yellow dress, just like she wore her yellow sunflower apron. I wore her purple apron and dress. Grandma would host tea parties, serving us hot chocolate in the little teacups from her collection. Just think—she likely sat in this very room sipping tea from the Daly china teacups with family and friends."

Everyone peered around envisioning the setting.

"She might have even dressed like us." Rachel brushed her satin-gloved hands down the front of her dress. "We'll have to take a promo shot of us in this room."

"We should be making a video advertising the event," Declan said. "That video of the Irish priest singing at the wedding a few years ago went viral."

"I can't sing," I said. "Besides, how would we get it to go viral?"

"Don't need it to be going viral," he said. "Just needs to be intriguing enough to grab people's attention. We could promote it on social media, targeting an audience within a hundred-mile radius."

A loud baaing noise carried through the library's open window.

"What the bloody hell?" Thomas raced toward the front door, and we followed.

I grasped the sides of my dress and raised it so I didn't trip going down the steps. I had slipped on a pair of George's backless slippers. I didn't want them to go flying off and me to go flying down like I had when running out of a Dublin hotel—in front of Brecker's CEO.

The entire family of sheep was at the shrubs. *David* was missing his private parts, and if the *Venus de Milo* hadn't already been missing both arms, she would have been now. Her one leg was toast.

"I swear I put the chain back on," I said.

Thomas ran at the sheep, yelling, his arms flapping, a barking Mac hot on his heels. We women hiked our dresses up to our knees. Me in my slippers, Mom in tennies, and Rachel in black riding boots. The five sheep went in different directions, so we separated, attempting to chase them toward the front entrance. The dress slipped from my grasp. I stepped on the bottom, and the sound of material ripping filled the air. Shit.

Mac was once again running circles around the sprawling lawn. It was hard to tell if he was chasing the sheep or they were chasing him. Thomas called out to Mac, directing him toward the gate. The dog amazingly obeyed, racing toward the entrance, the sheep following. Mac barked while Thomas scrambled to remove the chain. Once the gate was open, Mac rounded up the sheep and chased them out. As much as I despised Enid, I appreciated the fact that she'd helped Mac find his calling. Of course, I would never admit my gratitude.

We all bent over, hands on our legs, trying to catch our breath. Moments later a car drove up the road. Slowing down, the driver eyed us with interest. We all waved at the older man.

"Come back in two weeks," I hollered.

Declan smiled. "Intrigued to know more, isn't he now?"

Seized with inspiration, I said, "What if we go into towns dressed in costume to hand out flyers for the event? That will get people spreading the word."

Declan nodded. "Brilliant idea. And a video of what just happened would definitely go viral."

"Hmm..." I pondered.

Thomas shook his head. "No way in bloody hell are we letting those bastards back in here. This has Cousin Enid written all over it." He ran off to assess the damage to his shrubs.

"Ah, well," Declan said. "Couldn't reenact that scene if we wanted to, I suppose."

We exchanged mischievous glances.

Could we?

Mom checked my torn dress.

I peered over my shoulder, straining to see the tear. "How bad is it?"

"It's the seam. No worries. I'll be able to fix it."

We were almost to the house when a vintage sports car drove slowly up the drive—British racing green with a long, sleek hood, chrome grill, and rims. Fanny's blue hat and eyes were all that were visible over the dashboard, and her white-gloved hands grasped the steering wheel. We stepped onto the grass, and she gave us a wave as she passed by.

Declan let out a low whistle. "Fanny certainly isn't after George for his money. That's an antique Aston Martin. Like the original James Bond car. Worth several hundred thousand pounds, I'd say."

Go Fanny.

The woman parked and opened the car door. She swung her feet out of the vehicle, then slid off the tan leather seat. "Thought I'd bring a few things over to help decorate." She snatched a wicker basket off the front seat. "And I brought more scones for everyone."

I smiled. "Perfect."

"Pastor Alldridge didn't have time to search for George's baptismal record today, but he promised to do so."

Searching and *finding* were two different things.

The car's small backseat and trunk were filled with boxes and two Victorian-style lamps with dainty blue-and-pink floral-patterned shades accented with blue fringe. They'd go perfectly in George's blue bedroom but not so much the library. Yet, beggars couldn't be choosers. Declan, Rachel, and I hauled everything inside while Mom and Fanny discussed more menu ideas.

"Well, I best be going," Fanny said. "Need to keep spreading the word about the event." She slipped back behind the wheel of the sports car and puttered down the drive without having commented on our 1920s attire.

We went into the salon and each opened a box. Mine contained a few dozen perfume bottles, a jewelry box, and several framed photos. In one pic, Fanny wore a long blue dress and white fur stole, reclining on a pink velvet settee, with pink lips and rouge circles on her photoshopped wrinkle-free cheeks. It appeared the prim and proper Fanny had a risqué side. The box contained items you'd find on a bedroom dresser top, including a white lace dresser scarf. Hmm...

Mom carefully removed a delicate antique doll in a Victorian lace dress with a porcelain face and hands. "There's at least a dozen in here. I don't think we should put these out. The collection must be worth a fortune. It should be displayed in a china cabinet."

Rachel sniffed a bundle of three purple linen pouches tied together with a purple satin bow. "Lavender sachets. Like for dresser drawers or a closet."

Declan held up several historical romance novels with rather provocative covers. "Fanny trying to give George some not-so-subtle hints, is she?" He gestured to the perfume bottles. "Doesn't she need some of those yokes at home?"

I smiled. "I think she's hoping this will *be* her home when George returns from the hospital."

It appeared George might come home to discover he had a new roomie. However, sweet Fanny wanted to move in to care for George, whereas Cousin Enid wanted to move in so she could kick him out.

That evening Mom made platters of finger sandwiches, practicing for our afternoon tea. The bread was cut into various shapes filled with peanut butter and jelly, egg salad, and ham and cheese. She'd saved the crusts to dip in a container of hummus, refusing to waste food.

She'd just sat down on the library's couch to eat when her phone rang. "Your father has impeccable timing, as usual." She answered the call. "Hello, dear." She took a sip of tea. "There's no mac and cheese in the freezer. I have no idea what that might be. Have a sandwich. That's what we're eating." She let out a tired sigh and walked out of the room to take the call.

Rachel was sitting at the desk, wrapped in George's robe. She'd established an online account to accept credit cards for ticket sales and was now creating the event's website content. Brecker's web designer owed her a favor and was building the site. Fanny's blue lamps provided additional desktop lighting since half the chandelier bulbs were burned out.

The woman's historical romance novels filled two bookcase shelves along with her photos and Thomas's framed articles, documenting prestigious awards for his topiary. Mom had agreed to display the expensive china doll collection on a top shelf, safely out of reach. The rest of Fanny's personal items were boxed up. She and George could determine their placement.

I was attempting to write a one-minute promo video. If I was handwriting it rather than typing it on my laptop, the floor would be littered with crumpled sheets of paper. Besides the pressure of the video needing to sell tons of tickets, I needed it finished.

Tomorrow I had to work my day job, at least a half day. It would take me that long to figure out how to write a request for proposals from hotels in three countries. And I had to take the dreaded plunge into the white binder from hell and verify what documents were missing. That wouldn't be easy when I had no clue what it should contain. The upside to tomorrow being Monday was that Nicholas Turney was going to the registrar's office to search for Grandma's birth record.

My phone dinged. A text from Zoe. I'd contacted her that I wouldn't be home today but that she was more than welcome to stay at my place. I'd mentioned the art-mystery event.

Can't wait. I'll play a 1920s American film noir actress. No need to write me a part. I've got this. Send me a pic of my dress. Any purple ones? How fun!

The blue chiffon froufrou dress was likely the only one that would fit her slim figure.

She included a pic of her cat Quigley at the craft show, modeling their new summer line. A yellow crocheted sunflower hat framed Quigley's unhappy face. Poor Quigley. I prayed Zoe stuck with pet apparel and never knitted something she'd suck me in to modeling in public.

Declan walked in and dropped down on the couch next to me, rubbing his eyes. "Done for the night. My eyes are wrecked. All the paint is making me light-headed."

"I hope my mom wasn't meddling again when I went china shopping with Rachel."

He smiled. "She's grand. I'd be hugely protective too if I had a gorgeous daughter living *alone* in Dublin." He brushed a soft kiss to my lips. "Need help?"

I let out a frustrated groan. "I used to put on plays in our backyard all the time, but they were never posted on social media. Talk about pressure."

He slipped his phone from his jeans pocket. "Just ad lib. No need for a script." He started recording.

"I don't know if I could do that."

"Doing it right now, ya are. And you're dressed for it."

I'd tried my costume back on after Mom had sewed up the tear. It looked good as new.

Declan stood, offering me his hand. I grasped hold of it, and he pulled me up, directing me to the salon. Mac trotted behind, his claws clicking against the wood floor.

Declan slipped his arms around my waist and drew me snuggly against him. "You're wicked hot in this dress," he whispered in my ear, his warm breath sending a rush of heat through my chilled body. "But I'd prefer to be taking it off ya." He brushed his lips to my neck and swept a hand up my back. His fingers teased the zipper pull, and my breath caught in my throat.

I threw my arms around his neck and kissed him until we were out of breath. When I finally came up for air, I drew back slightly. A mischievous glint twinkled in his blue eyes.

"We might have to find a deserted road to go parking tomorrow or send my mom and Rachel into town on errands." Mac distracted me, batting around a black object next to the fireplace. "What is that?"

Declan peered over at the dog. "I found some catch-and-release mouse traps in Lancaster today. Hid them around the house."

I wanted to rip his clothes off right here in the salon.

He scolded Mac and tucked the small black cylinder tube next to the fireplace.

Mac let out a bark, pawing at Declan's phone in his hand.

"What?" Declan said. "Want to star in the video, do ya?"

Mac wagged his tail.

"Brilliant idea. People go mad over animals in commercials. But no self-respecting dog in the 1920s would have worn a green tutu. Animal lovers weren't as crazy back then."

"Good luck with that."

"You distract him, and I'll slip it off."

I removed the purple lilacs from the vase on the fireplace mantel. I held them in front of Mac. While the dog frantically sniffed the lilacs, Declan swiftly stripped off the tutu. Mac spun around and growled at him. He jumped up, trying to snag the tulle garment from Declan's hand. Declan tossed me the tutu like a hot potato.

"Oh sure, get me involved." I tossed it back.

Mom walked in the front door, having finished her call. She clapped her hands, and all three of us jumped. She held out her hand. I gave her the tutu. Mac growled at it.

Mom gave Mac a stern look. "You don't talk to your grandmother that way."

Mac stopped growling and sat.

"You really need to teach him some manners." She walked into the library with the tutu.

I needed to teach him *anything*.

Declan positioned me in front of the two paintings on the wall, next to an empty screw. Mac sat at my feet. Declan started filming, and I froze, seized by stage fright.

"I don't think I can act on demand."

"Used to produce plays, didn't ya?"

"I produced more than acted in them. Pretending like the theft just happened might make people think there was another one. And if I say there's been a break in the case, they might also believe that."

"Seeing as you're wearing a vintage dress, I think people will be realizing a theft didn't just occur. Make a plea for help with cracking the cold case. And a sexy British accent would make it more authentic." He wore a sly grin.

"I can't talk in a British accent."

"Right, then, forget the accent and just talk very proper and serious. Speak from your heart. You're passionate about saving the estate, and the only way to do that is to find the blokes who nicked the paintings." He framed the air with his hands. "Who locked you up in the loo. Ya can do this for George's sake. Not only are we rooting for George but against that bloody Enid. Don't want to be letting her win, do ya?"

A growl vibrated at the back of my throat. Mac barked.

I smiled, and Declan began recording.

CHAPTER THIRTEEN

After lying in bed all night listening to rain drip into the silver bucket, anticipating water gushing from the ceiling, I got up at 4:00 a.m., deciding to get a jump start on my busy day.

Despite the space heater in the bathroom, I was too cold to shower, and I didn't want to wake up Mom. I tossed my hair up in a clip but took time for mascara so Declan didn't think I'd let myself go since arriving in England. I quietly threw on jeans and Declan's blue wool sweater over a long-sleeved blue tee and wrapped my mohair scarf around my neck. I needed to cut the fingertips off my gloves so I could wear them while typing.

When I entered the library, I swore I could see my breath. Frost covered the bottom of the windows. However, no snow blanketed Thomas's purple and pink peonies in the garden. Although it was dark out, moonlight cast a faint light over the frosted grounds, giving it a serene, though cold, look.

Shivering, I walked over to the fireplace. I'd never built a fire but had seen Declan do it many times. I stacked kindling, then strategically placed wood on top of it. I lit the kindling, and flames shot up. Holding my hands near the fire, I rubbed them together, the feeling slowly returning to my fingers.

Maybe I *could* be *Little Caity on the Bog* after all.

I booted my laptop and pulled up the website for Ireland's civil records. Having spent so much time on the site, I could navigate it with my eyes closed. Baptismal records for Killybog were only available online until 1900, and merely an index listed civil records. I searched for Grandma's birth record for the millionth time, checking alternate birth years, name spellings, anything that might be a lead. Dozens of female Coffey birth certificates in County Westmeath were missing first names and parents' names. Precisely why Nicholas Turney needed to view the original records at the registrar's office today. My chest fluttered, and I crossed my fingers for good luck.

An hour later I was perusing Canada's 1861 census, trying to locate Bernice and Gracie's McKinney family. After murdering the surname every way possible, I still couldn't find it. I opened the 1871 census I'd attached to James McKinney's family tree on Ancestry.com. I viewed the scrawled handwriting on the original image, reconfirming it was the correct family.

I scanned the page, zoning in on a Richard McKinney living three houses away with Rebecca Hale, a widow. Richard was sixteen, two years older than James's brother John McKinney. Had *Richard* been the oldest son, not *John*? Had he been living with a widowed aunt or rellie? McKinney was an uncommon name. I was ecstatic at the possibility yet wanted to beat my head against the desk in frustration. I'd spent a hundred hours searching Scotland's records for a James McKinney born to a John and Mary in the Glasgow area. I hadn't found it because it likely didn't exist. I was fairly certain there'd been a James born to a Richard. Ugh!

Mom walked into the room wearing her robe and glasses, startling me. "It's only six. What are you doing up?"

"Couldn't sleep. Just doing a bit of research."

She stood over by the fireplace. "Good job with the fire. Some tea might also help warm us up. Would you like some, and one of Fanny's scones?"

"A lemon poppy seed would be great."

Mom went to the kitchen to make breakfast. We really needed to learn how to operate that massive cast-iron stove. It could probably heat the entire house in five minutes flat.

As much as I wanted to pursue this new McKinney lead, I couldn't get sucked in to genealogy research when I needed to work on my day job.

By 9:00 a.m., I'd downed six cups of tea and eaten three lemon poppy seed scones. High on caffeine, my fingers were flying across the keyboard. I'd booked a Dublin restaurant for the twenty-person meeting at the Connelly Court Hotel in two weeks. Found a template for requesting hotel proposals on a planners' forum. After going through the binder, I determined that last year's hotel contract was missing and contacted the hotel for a copy. I was currently typing away as Declan fired off hotel and venue recommendations for Florence and Dubrovnik. Surprisingly, Rachel was still in bed, so now was the time to pick Declan's brain.

"Planners are always asking me for recommendations. You shouldn't hesitate to ask Rachel about the contracts. I've never negotiated one. I haven't a clue about group rates."

"I'll negotiate provisions based on last year's contract. Once I get it from the hotel." I glared at the massive binder on the desk, which was undoubtedly missing more than the contract. "The rates will just be different."

"Accounting for fluctuating exchange rates might be a wee bit of a challenge. Croatia isn't on the euro."

Lovely. One more issue to deal with.

"How do you spell that villa in Italy?" I asked.

"What villa in Italy?" Rachel shuffled into the library in George's red wool slippers, tightening the sash on his navy robe. She plopped down on the couch with her laptop.

"Nothing, just chatting."

Declan left me with a kiss to begin his third painting.

"I can't believe you slept in."

"Didn't go to bed until after two. Finished the website. We just need to test it this morning before we start promoting it. I also created a flyer to hand out in town today." She eyed the printer under the desk, which looked like it should be housed in the Smithsonian. "If that doesn't work, we'll find a place to have them printed."

"Wow, you did have a busy night."

She nodded. "Where's Mom?"

"Took Mac for a walk. Will probably have him fully trained by the time they return. And Thomas is outside redesigning his damaged shrubs." I cringed at the thought of David's missing body parts.

"Did you talk to your boss yet?"

I shrugged. "It's Monday. He probably has loads of e-mails to get through and calls to make."

"He's the CEO. He checks e-mail and voicemail twenty-four seven. You can't put this off."

"Okay. I'll do it now."

Rachel sat there, watching me.

"I can't call with you listening."

"Fine." She dragged herself up from the couch. "I'll go grab something to eat." She walked past me, her gaze narrowing on my computer screen. "Is that my VIP suite checklist?"

"Yeah, I was just looking through my file of meeting notes."

She squinted at the screen. "You have twenty-three pages of planner notes?" She sounded impressed. "That's great. That's how you learn, by watching other planners and asking questions."

Maybe I *should* ask Rachel for some hotel suggestions...

"Even though I wasn't happy about you going for the job, I know you can do it. I'm proud of you for landing it on your own merit."

Rachel was proud of me?

It wasn't a warning disguised as a compliment that I better not mess up. But it convinced me even more that I couldn't ask her for assistance on the Europe incentive after she'd said *on my own merit*. And made me more worried about her reaction when she discovered I hadn't started the citizenship process after assuring my boss it was a given.

She pointed to the white binder. "That's insanely huge."

Rachel stored meeting documents in a computer file but kept paper backup copies for critical ones like contracts... Which she also kept on Brecker's network drive... A drive I had access to. I didn't have to ask Rachel for help. I could review her contracts online. Not like I'd be hacking into her computer system. I had legitimate access. Yet it still seemed wrong to not ask her, and what if she could tell I'd accessed the files?

Rachel headed toward the door.

"If you've run out of energy drinks, there's a stash in the cupboard by the fridge." I was going to be hitting them before this day was done.

"I still have some cold ones. Trying to cut back. Figured vacation would be a good time to wean myself off."

Seriously?

Speed-dialing my boss, I took an encouraging breath, peering out the window at the rain watering the pink and purple peonies. I stifled a yawn right when my boss answered the call.

I explained my circumstances.

"Family comes first," he said.

"I'll be working from here. I've started the ball rolling on the Europe incentive, checking hotel rates and availability."

"Decided to hold a June meeting with our brewery in Kerry, either at the Ballyseede or Ballygarry hotels.

They're both popular, so we need to move on it straight away. I'll give it to Gemma to plan."

After the wench had stolen the St Patrick's Day event, no way in hell was she staying at a castle when I was glamping! I assured him I could handle it and crossed my fingers that I wouldn't have been deported by then.

"I don't want you overwhelmed when you're new to the position and have family issues to tend to."

He sounded like my mom.

"I can handle it," I said.

"If you're sure..."

What did I need to do to gain this guy's confidence?

We said good-bye, and I sat there with the phone to my ear, staring out at Thomas in his wellies and green rain gear, walking through the garden. Why hadn't I let my boss hand the new meeting off to Gemma? I didn't have time for another project. But I needed to prove myself.

An e-mail popped in my inbox from Mindy. She had some great suggestions for Dubrovnik. Some of her Florence recommendations matched Declan's. Same as Declan, she didn't negotiate contracts, so she wasn't familiar with hotels' average group rates. I might have to break down and ask Rachel to review them. This had to be a killer program. Mindy was in Barcelona working a program from hell with Blair, the planner I'd worked with in Prague.

Weren't all of Blair's programs hell?

And to think I'd almost signed on for her May meeting in Monte Carlo. I cringed at the thought.

I'd never seen the *Blair Witch Project.*
I'd lived it.

❧ ❧

Late morning we went into Dalwick to promote the event. Declan set up his easel next to the quaint stone bridge across from Nicole's Vintage Finds. A pic of one of the stolen paintings was clipped to the top of the easel. Declan wore black slacks, a white button-down shirt with rolled-up sleeves, and George's red ascot tied loosely around the shirt's crisp collar. He'd actually ironed for the occasion. A clump of hair fell over his forehead while he painted with dramatic enthusiasm, capturing the attention of passersby.

I fought the urge to rip off his ascot and shirt.

God, I loved that man.

Rachel waved a hand in front of my face. I dragged my gaze from Declan to my sister in the champagne-colored dress and matching long satin gloves. Wearing high heels, the bottom of her dress came just shy of touching the ground. The rain had stopped, but we'd have to avoid puddles. Dry cleaning was not in our budget.

"Why don't you stay here and hand out flyers so Declan doesn't have to stop painting to do it. Mom and I'll walk around town and drop some off at the gallery."

"Sounds like a plan."

A couple was already asking Mom about her burgundy dress and fancy black hat with the gold brooch.

I straightened the green feathers in my headband and secured it in place with a bobby pin. I smoothed a nervous hand over the embroidered jade dress, while Mac relaxed on the grass, sunning himself, not a care in the world.

People were out and about for lunch, so I blew through most of my flyers in an hour. Declan and I were getting ready to pack up and move on to Lancaster when a woman's voice shrilled through the air. Our gazes darted to Cousin Enid marching across the street in rhino mode, dressed in dark-green breeches, a green tweed jacket, and brown riding boots.

"What do you think you are doing?" she demanded, her stern tone causing several curious people to stop and watch. Her gaze narrowed on Declan's painting of the stolen artwork, and she gasped in horror. She glared at my dress. "Where did you get that?"

"None of your business."

"I beg to differ. I know precisely where you stole that from. The theater group."

"We didn't steal it."

She attempted to snag the band off my head, a feather catching in my hair. She gave it a tug, pulling my hair.

Mac let out a bark.

"Ouch," I yelped, grasping hold of the band so she couldn't yank it again. I'd won two catfights in junior high. I didn't plan on losing this one. I gave Enid's hand a firm squeeze. She let out a squeal and released the band. I blew the feather from my eyes and adjusted the band on my head, trying to regain my composure.

Nicole ran across the street, and the crowd parted, allowing her access to the fighting ring. "What's going on?"

"That dress belongs to the theater." Enid's gray eyes about bugged out of her head as Rachel and Mom marched up. "So do those."

"I borrowed the dresses for an event they're holding, along with some furniture and props. None of the actors had an issue with it."

"Well, I certainly take issue with it." She peered over at us. "Remove those costumes immediately."

"I'm not stripping in the middle of town," I said.

"Are ya mad?" Declan asked.

"I am a major contributor to the theater, and I will not stand for this. You shall return those at once, or I'm cutting off all funding." She removed an envelope from her purse and held it out. Mac snatched it from her, and she snapped her hand back. "Better watch your mutt, or I'll be suing you next. Give that to George and advise him he's being sued for my share of our family's fortune."

Enid glared at Mac scratching away at the cobblestone-paved bridge, attempting to bury the letter. "Not a very bright creature, is he? Well, he can eat it, and it won't matter. I'll still be suing."

Rachel got in Enid's face. "You're not getting away with this."

The woman pursed her lips, then spun around on her bootheels and marched off.

Nicole shook her head. "Slag."

"I'm so sorry," I said. "We'll return the outfits."

"You will not. We're fed up with her holier-than-thou

attitude, acting like she owns the theater group. However, she's likely hiring a truck right now to move the furniture or to barricade the entrance. Sorry."

"Are you sure about the costumes?" I said.

She gave a definitive nod. "Absolutely." Spotting customers heading into her shop, she excused herself.

We took advantage of the crowd and gave our spiel and handed out flyers before they dispersed.

"Looks like we'll be the hot gossip." Declan smirked. "That lady's tantrum backfired on her."

Mom adjusted the band on my head. "She's no lady. She's a...bitch."

Rachel and I exchanged shocked looks. We'd only heard Mom swear once. When Rachel and I had gotten into her makeup and resembled cheap hookers rather than the beauty-pageant look we were going for. She'd yelled, "What the hell are you doing in my makeup!" Never having heard her swear, Rachel and I burst into tears and ran into our bedrooms. We buried our faces in the pillows, smearing red lipstick all over them, making Mom even more furious. But not as furious as when I proceeded to cry so hard I puked all over my bedspread.

Declan curled his fingers into fists. "If our car was big enough, I'd be driving over there right now and collecting the furniture before she could take it."

"And you know she will." I growled. "Where are we going to get couches and chairs for free?" I glanced down to find Mac burying the envelope in the dirt. I snatched it up and gave him a pat on the head. "Wish it were that easy, fella."

"Yeah, maybe we should bury that *woman* instead," Mom said.

Wow. This from the *woman* who used to tell us, *You might not like someone much, but you should never say you hate her.* That was her advice after we'd had a fight at school. And I'd respond, *Then I wish she was dead.* Needless to say, that never went over well.

"Now you know how I felt about Missy Puetz." My archenemy in sixth grade.

Mom nodded. "She was a snotty little brat."

And so the truth comes out.

CHAPTER
FOURTEEN

After distributing flyers in Lancaster, we stopped by to visit George. Everyone agreed it was best not to leave flyers at the hospital so staff didn't tell George about the event rather than us. We told the curious nurse at the reception desk that our 1920s attire was for a historical reenactment, which was the truth. She advised us that George was being prepped to have the fluid removed from his lungs.

"What if he doesn't make it through surgery?" Mom said.

"It's not a major surgery, merely a brief procedure." The nurse gave Mom a reassuring smile.

"How long will it take?" I asked.

"About a half hour. Depending on when the doctor begins, you should be able to visit him in an hour or two."

"Should we come back?" Rachel asked.

Mom dropped down onto a chair. "I'm not leaving until he's out of surgery."

The nurse directed us to a waiting room down the hall with vending machines and complimentary coffee and tea. I sipped tea and munched on cheese-and-onion potato chips while watching some hideous soap opera in which every character should win a Razzie Award for worst actor. Yet we watched three back-to-back episodes before the nurse returned.

"The procedure went well. His breathing is already a bit better. He's in his room, resting peacefully. And he's awake."

We shot up from our chairs.

"He's awake?" Mom said.

The nurse nodded. "But he's quite tired and a bit incoherent."

Mom smiled wide. "But he's awake."

We bolted down the hall to George's room.

George was lying in an upright position against the bed, looking groggy, head bobbing from side to side. No longer wearing an oxygen mask, he was reciting the nursery rhyme, "Hickory Dickory Dock." His speech was slurred, his voice raspy from days without drinking water or talking. He was using Grandma's brooch to imitate a mouse crawling down his leg. It reminded me of the times I was high on laughing gas at the dentist.

Mom walked cautiously over to the bed, not wanting to startle him. "George, it's Barbara, Caity, Rachel, and Declan."

He peered at her through heavy lids. "I know that."

We thought he was referring to knowing *us*, until he began reciting "Georgie Porgie." "Georgie Porgie pudding...and pie"—he gasped for a breath—"kissed the girls..." His gaze narrowed while he searched for the words.

"And made them cry," Mom said.

"When the boys came out to play," Rachel, Declan, and I joined in. "Georgie Porgie ran away."

George closed his eyes and drifted off to sleep.

Mom smiled, despite the concerned look on her face. "Well, wasn't that fun?"

More like totally bizarre, but we all nodded.

After leaving the hospital, Mom decided we needed more charcoal. It wasn't easy finding briquettes in England's off-season. Grilling probably wasn't a popular pastime even in the summer, with all the rain. We'd had to stop at two fuel-oil companies and a garden shop to find eight bags.

England was about to have a run on charcoal.

Mom hadn't said a word about George's odd behavior since we'd left the hospital. We were almost to the estate when she burst into tears.

"Omigod, Mom, what's wrong?" Rachel scooted over next to Mom in the backseat and slipped an arm around her shoulder.

Declan and I exchanged worried looks. I crawled over the front seat and into the back with them.

"What if he has brain damage?" Mom removed a tissue from her purse. "All of his breathing problems and meds might have caused a lack of oxygen to his brain. Marjorie's husband had some memory loss and mobility issues after suffering a severe case of pneumonia. He was never right again."

Marjorie's husband had been a bit off prior to the pneumonia, but that was beside the point.

"I'm sure the nurse would have told us if they had any concerns with George's behavior," Rachel said.

I nodded. "Yeah. She said the procedure went great. And that other nurse mentioned he's been coming to for a bit at night but hasn't been real coherent."

"Maybe the doctors don't know what George was like *before* the pneumonia." Mom peered at me through tear-filled eyes. "He wasn't like that when you two met, was he?"

I shook my head. "Of course not. He's going to be fine. I'm sure he is."

When we pulled up to the gate, no sheep lurked around. I hopped out of the car and opened the gate using the key Thomas had given us after a locksmith fixed it that morning. I stood guard while Declan pulled in and then secured the lock. We headed up the drive. Thomas was still performing cosmetic surgery on his damaged artwork, attaching limbs from the shrubs fully intact.

David now had prosthetic private parts.

"Jaysus," Declan muttered, grimacing. "That looks massively painful, and it's only a shrub."

"I don't think we should mention our visit to Thomas," Mom said. "Our nursery-rhyme recital might worry him."

We all agreed.

I told Thomas about our confrontation with Cousin Enid and the letter on Edwards and Price stationary advising George he was being sued.

Thomas tightened his grasp on the hedge clipper's wooden handles and sliced the blades through the air, almost snipping off David's new private parts. An inspired look seized his face.

Cousin Enid was toast.

"Why didn't I think of this sooner? There's furniture in the shed. There might be something of use. George hadn't yet been desperate enough to dig through the mess back there. It's been a dumping ground for years."

A *dumping ground* didn't sound real promising.

We followed Thomas out to one of several stone buildings behind the house.

"Do you think there are mice in there?" Rachel asked.

There were mice in the *house.*

Thomas smiled. "They are more afraid of you than you are of them."

"I doubt that," she said.

He opened the door, and a damp, musty smell poured out. He brushed away the cobwebs stretched across the doorway. No electricity, merely a few dirty windows provided light. He propped the door open with a chair.

"Only a few more hours of daylight, so we best be quick."

Occasional tables, lamps, assorted wooden chairs, stacks of boxes and crates, and odds and ends filled the building. A porcelain figurine of a two-headed camel sat on a bronze table with a base that resembled a flying monkey from *The Wizard of Oz.* Next to it stood a wooden carving of a man wearing merely a seashell necklace, with big eyes and small feet, dancing. The items looked like souvenirs from the Daly family's exotic travels. Only the person who'd schlepped them thousands of miles home had cared enough to display them, so eventually everything had made its way to the shed.

Thomas pointed out a wooden cuckoo clock with deer antlers on the top. "A friend brought that back from Germany for Isabella Daly. We weren't allowed to play with it. Had supposedly been purchased at an antique shop and of some value. It was one of only five made with the cuckoo bird upside down. Diana thought it was hideous and stuck it out here."

Too bad the *Antiques Roadshow* wasn't in town.

"Maybe we could convince Cousin Enid it's a treasured family heirloom. Along with that." Rachel gestured to a demented-looking stuffed owl.

"And the flying monkey table," I said.

Declan nodded. "She can be taking it back to Oz with her."

I smiled. "I was thinking the same thing."

We were so in sync.

Mom walked over to a cradle with ornately crafted wooden spindles and headboard. Chewed-out stuffing and mouse droppings covered the soiled mattress. Rachel glanced around for small critters. Mom placed a hand on the side and gently rocked it.

"This must have been George's." She wore a melancholy expression as if imagining Grandma rocking George to sleep. "Wonder if he'd mind you girls using this when you have children."

I avoided Declan's gaze. We weren't to the point of discussing children, except Mac. And if we couldn't discipline a dog, how would we ever control kids? Besides, did Declan even want kids? He'd commented in Paris about having no desire to deal with zippies and nappies, but had he been serious or had Little Henry, the VIP's kid I'd played nanny to, temporarily soured his opinion on children?

"I'm sure he'd love that," Thomas said.

We divided and searched through the clutter.

"I found books," Rachel called out. "Enough to fill at least one bookcase in the library."

"A few charcoal briquettes and nobody will know they've been stored in a shed for decades," Mom said. "Certainly don't want the house to smell any mustier than it does."

We ended up with twenty-three boxes of books, three cocktail and occasional tables, fourteen assorted wooden chairs, and a slew of eclectic décor we'd use if we were desperate, which I had the feeling we would be.

&❧ ❧&

We didn't eat dinner until almost nine. The meal included tuna fish on little croissant rolls, cucumber and cream cheese on rye bread, and peanut butter and jelly. I sat at the library desk sipping tea from my pink English cottage teacup, eating peanut butter and jelly sandwiches, and checking e-mail. Declan was in the foyer painting. Rachel was on the couch, wrapped up in George's robe, typing away on her laptop. And Mom, in her velour robe, was sitting on the floor in front of the fireplace, wiping down books. Some books had been stored in vintage wooden milk crates that read *Lancaster Dairy*, while others appeared to have been stashed in the shed more recently in cardboard boxes. Mom replaced the cleaned books into a crate with charcoal briquettes on a piece of aluminum foil.

An e-mail from Nicholas Turney popped into my inbox.

He'd come up empty at Mullingar's registrar's office. No birth certificate on file for Grandma, at least not one that had been correctly documented. I collapsed back against the chair with an overwhelming sense of defeat, despite Nicholas's pep talk to not give up hope. Tomorrow he planned to visit Catholic churches near Killybog and review baptismal records.

I needed to go to a church and light a few dozen candles.

Maybe I could visit George's church and check on his baptismal record. Fanny hadn't mentioned if the pastor had found it. Was there a reason I hadn't asked about it and that Fanny hadn't gotten back to me? If Grandma's and Michael's names weren't on the baptismal certificate, would I share the truth, or would it be Fanny's and my secret? But why would George's mom have lied on her deathbed—when she'd confessed that his biological mother was Bridget Coffey, my grandma, and his birth father was John Michael Daly? Maybe she hadn't lied but had been babbling incoherently like George had today...

I shoved the thoughts aside and opened an e-mail from Mindy, which included ideas for our art-mystery event. She thought someone should get killed and die a slow, painful death. Like maybe with a paintbrush to the heart. Her program with Blair was apparently getting worse.

"Have you checked ticket sales?" I asked Rachel.

"Two more than the last time you asked, fifteen minutes ago. So that puts us at ten. Not bad for just going live today."

"I'd expected more after Enid's scene in town. Maybe we should stalk her tomorrow and cause an even bigger one."

"Word will spread," Mom said. "It'll just take time."

We didn't have time.

I tried to focus on work and not have a panic attack over all the problems bombarding my head. What if George had lost oxygen to his brain and the only thing he and Mom would have to discuss was their love of childhood nursery rhymes? What if the event didn't succeed and George lost the estate? Could Enid really sue over the family belongings being sold? Would I be able to sleep tonight without having confirmed Richard had indeed been James McKinney's oldest son? And why wasn't I as concerned about my Flanagan job as I was about everything else?

"I need to get away from this computer before I go blind." Rachel set her laptop on the cocktail table and joined Mom in wiping down books.

A half hour later, I was sending a request for a proposal to a Vienna hotel when Rachel gasped.

"Omigod." She stared at the inside cover of a mauve cloth-covered book. "Happy Christmas to my dearest Michael. I will forever love you. Bridget." She handed Mom the book. "It's dated 1935. It had to be Grandma's."

"A year before Michael died," I said, sitting next to them on the floor.

The cover had fancy gilt lettering in the center of an ivy emblem. *A Christmas Carol* by Charles Dickens.

Mom nodded. "It's her handwriting."

"What if it's a first edition?" Rachel pointed at the roman numerals on the cover page. "I have no clue what year that is. It's in great shape, besides the slightly worn edges and the cover being a bit faded. Why would she have left the book here? And why did they store such a valuable book in a shed?"

"Maybe the book wasn't that valuable in the 1930s," I said.

Mom slammed the cover shut. "Because she left behind everything of value to her. Even if it wasn't of high monetary value." She tossed the book aside.

"We can't sell it," I said.

Mom nodded. "We will if needed."

"The writing on the cover page might decrease the value," Rachel said.

It was priceless to me. No way were we going to get desperate enough to sell that book.

"I've been talking and working so fast, I haven't been paying any attention to titles," Mom said.

We went back through several boxes of books. Other than a first-edition *Mary Poppins*, we didn't recognize many of the titles or authors. Based on a Google search, the Dickens book was a third edition published in 1843. Estimates varied widely depending on the condition, but it seemed likely it was worth at least five grand. I still refused to sell it. Most boxes and crates had been stored on top of furnishings, having protected them from water damage. The books were in good shape except for the slightly musty smell Mom was convinced the charcoal would eliminate. It would take a while to examine twenty-three boxes of them.

"We'll be lucky to get what they're worth since we don't have time to put them on eBay and wait for a bidding war," Rachel said. "We need to find local book dealers or an auction house."

A chill raced through me, and I snuggled into Declan's wool sweater. I glanced over at the flames dancing around in the fireplace. "Are you guys cold?"

"You mean colder than usual?" Rachel said.

"It does seem a bit chillier." Mom rubbed the sleeves of her velour robe.

I went out to the salon to ask Declan's opinion on the temp, Mac following.

Declan walked in from the dining room. "The thermostat reads ten Celsius. Boiler must be banjaxed."

"We'll have to take turns getting up during the night to make fires, or we can all sleep huddled around the space heater from the bathroom. Don't want everyone getting sick."

There went any earnings from the sale of books, and we'd all end up with pneumonia to boot. Running an English estate was turning out to be one step up from glamping.

I let out a frustrated sigh. "What's next?"

A squeal pierced the air. "A mouse!" Rachel screamed.

Declan grabbed Mac's collar so he couldn't run and catch it, if Rachel hadn't already given it a heart attack.

I really needed to stop saying *What's next.*

"Shit! There're two!"

I needed to even stop *thinking* it!

CHAPTER FIFTEEN

We'd been sheep-free, mice-free, and Enid-free for two days. The wretched woman certainly hadn't given up trying to sabotage the event and George's life. She was probably deep in the trenches determining her next tactical move. I welcomed whatever she wanted to throw at us. Her interference was turning out to be quite motivating.

Rachel's meltdown had freaked out the mice, and they'd raced for cover under the couch, straight into one of the humane mouse houses. Declan released them at the edge of the property. It would be lovely if they, or their family and friends, didn't find their way back inside before the event.

George was still quite weak and sleeping through the days, except for a brief period yesterday. The nurse called early afternoon, and we raced over to the hospital to find he'd fallen back to sleep. I was actually relieved, not wanting another nursery-rhyme incident to dampen Mom's spirits and worry her even more. We hadn't spoken about the episode since her meltdown in the car.

Rachel and Mom had sold the more valuable books to a dealer in Lancaster and made enough to replace the boiler. At least the unexpected expense hadn't had to come out of the event's profit. It was one less thing for George to worry about when he got home from the hospital. Mom hadn't searched for Grandma's book when they'd taken the others to sell, so that was a good sign. The book was tucked away in my suitcase. I wasn't giving it up unless we were desperate. George should keep it. The books of no monetary value helped fill the library's empty shelves.

Money flowed in from the upcoming events. The Saturday evening ones were almost sold out, and the others were filling up fast, thanks to Enid's scene in Dalwick and the video promo. Declan was savvy about Facebook ads, having assisted a client with them. I'd insisted he use my credit card as he was fronting the money for all the paintings. I'd get reimbursed after the event, before my payment was due.

The video had over ten thousand likes and several hundred comments. I'd only had time to read a few. An elderly man in Manchester thought my dress was lovely and wondered if I wanted to wear it to the opera with him at the end of the month. A woman asked where I had my hair colored. Um, my hair was a natural auburn. And a marketing company offered a discount to produce our video trailer. How rude. With over ten thousand likes, did it look like we needed their services?

I held the front door while Thomas and Declan

hauled Fanny's blue velvet couch inside. Mac was sprawled out on the matching love seat in the salon, his head resting on a frilly lace pillow. Her blue upholstered wingback chair sat in a corner, the flying monkey table next to it, displaying a vintage book and teacup. The table was starting to grow on me, but Mac growled every time he passed it. I could picture George sitting in the chair, wearing his robe and slippers, smoking a pipe, reading a book. If Rachel would give up his robe and slippers. A navy-and-cream-patterned rug, also Fanny's, covered most of the wooden floor, giving the room a much cozier feel. Ireland was known for forty shades of green. Fanny was known for forty shades of blue.

I feared her bedroom set might be next. No way could poor Thomas help haul that up the stairs, and a bed wouldn't be appropriate for people to sit on at afternoon tea. Those would be my excuses for turning away the woman's bedroom furnishings. It appeared that Fanny had lost sight of the original purpose for her *loaning* us the furniture.

The elderly lady was humming a happy tune while she placed lace doilies on the arms of the wingback chair.

Declan and Thomas set the couch down in the salon for a quick breather. Next, they were using Thomas's friend's truck and trailer to pick up furniture from theater group members. When they'd heard about Cousin Enid banning us from using the theater props, many of the actors offered to loan us their personal furniture. By the end of the day, the library would comfortably seat fifty.

Declan sniffed the air. "That smell reminds me of my mum hanging sheets out to dry on the line."

I nodded. "It's Fanny's vanilla- and linen-scented candles."

And a couple hundred pounds of charcoal throughout the house had done wonders to diminish the musty smell and remove some of the dampness.

I plopped down on the couch between Declan and Thomas. Declan slipped an arm around my shoulder, and I snuggled against him. We admired the nine paintings hanging on the wall. Reproductions of the eight stolen ones and one that Thomas said had been George's favorite.

"Could have captured the sunlight better in that one, I'd say." Declan gestured to the painting of the woman at the desk writing a letter. "May need to touch it up a wee bit..."

"No way. You captured the sunlight perfectly. It warms me up every time I look at it."

"I believe that is my favorite also," Thomas said. "She's writing a letter to her lover, a duke."

"Really?" I said.

Thomas smiled. "That was always my story. Her expression is serene yet wistful as if she's wondering when they will once again see each other. George felt she was corresponding with a sister, sharing secrets. He always longed for a sibling. I was the closest thing he had to a brother. As he was to me." Thomas's eyes watered.

I placed a comforting hand on his arm. "He's going to recover now that they drained the fluid from his lungs." Thankfully, we hadn't told Thomas about our visit with George. It would have upset him as much as it had Mom.

Thomas nodded, staring reminiscently at the painting.

Needing to finish some work before lunch, I left the guys to rest and went to the library. I was creating a database with the eleven hotel quotes I'd received. Dubrovnik was coming in at the lowest cost. I'd printed off the contracts rather than having to navigate between a dozen open pages on my laptop.

Rachel walked in and set a plate of finger sandwiches on the desk, along with an energy drink. "What are you working on?" She snagged a hotel contract from the pile. "Dubrovnik?"

A nervous feeling fluttered in my chest. "Yeah. They're considering it for an incentive in August."

She scanned the contract. "Make sure they add a no-walk clause and give you a catering discount."

"I don't think either were in last year's contract."

I handed her the previous contract. She'd brought it up. Not like I'd been asking for help.

Rachel rolled her eyes. "That Joyce was as clueless as ditzy Gemma. They're meeting planner wannabees. They have no idea how to negotiate a contract."

That made three of us.

"I'll e-mail you some of the international contracts I've done recently. They'll list the provisions you need to include. Why didn't you just ask me to look this over?" Rachel sounded offended I hadn't requested her help.

"I didn't want you to think I was in over my head."

"Caity, I *know* you're in over your head. But like I've

said, that's how most planners learn. It took me dozens of contracts to figure out what I was doing. And I didn't have anyone to teach me."

My phone rang. George's hospital.

Heart racing, I answered the call.

After a brief conversation, I hung up. "George is awake."

Rachel let out a nervous laugh. "What's it today? 'Hey Diddle Diddle' or 'Humpty Dumpty'?"

I shook my head. "She says he's coherent."

We both let out a huge sigh of relief.

Rachel smiled. "Can't wait to meet our uncle."

⁂

When we entered the hospital room, George was lying in bed with his eyes closed. The framed photo of Mom and her family rested on his chest.

Mom smiled at the photo and whispered, "Maybe we should go to the cafeteria and come back in a bit."

Mac barked.

"Shh," we all said.

The dog trotted over to the bed. He slipped a paw through the bed's guardrail and placed it on George's hand. George's eyes slowly opened, and he peered at Mac through heavy lids. Fanny grasped hold of my arm, her face lighting up.

"Well, hello there, little fella. Who would you be?"

"Our newest family member, Mac," I said.

Not as new as George though.

Mac eyed the bed, preparing to jump up.

I clapped my hands like Mom always did. "Mac, come here."

Amazingly, he trotted over to me. Wow. Mom training him in a matter of days would save me a ton of money on obedience school.

George smiled, a twinkle in his gray eyes, a bit of pink glow back in his sunken cheeks. I introduced him to Rachel, Mom, and Declan.

Tearing up, Mom walked over and placed a hand on George's. "I can't believe I have a brother."

"And I a sister, or rather sisters."

"Dottie and Teri wished they could have made it, but they'll be joining me this summer."

"I hope to be back to my old self by then. Although I haven't been my old self for some time." He peered over at me. "You must think me a terrible and foolish old man for not having told you about the estate. Things moved rather quickly since we met in Prague. I didn't foresee it being to the point of selling so soon, and I felt I should tell you in person. You'd been so thrilled at the prospect of visiting where your grandmother had once lived. I was ashamed to admit I was losing it."

"You don't owe us an explanation." Mom patted his hand. "We just wished we'd known so we could have helped you save the estate sooner. And I plan to stay as long as you need me to."

"Save the estate?" George's forehead wrinkled in confusion.

We all nodded, anxious to fill him in on the event.

Thomas told him about Cousin Enid's deal with the law firm and their plan to turn his home into solicitor offices. We didn't want to upset him, but once Enid caught wind George was awake, she'd be here serving papers.

George's gaze narrowed with interest. "How much are they offering?"

"Ah, well, not sure," Thomas sputtered, as surprised by George's inquisitive and calm reaction as I was.

I'd expected him to be furious with his cousin and devastated that the buyer's former partner had run off with his wife and the estate's money.

I described the art-mystery event and assured him that ticket sales would enable him to turn down the law firm's offer.

A panicked look seized George's features. "Why would you plan such an event?"

My stomach dropped. Precisely the reaction I'd feared. George was freaking out over the mere thought of reliving that evening.

"I thought it was a brilliant idea," Thomas said. "That it would allow us both to have closure with what happened."

"I don't need closure," George spat. "Or people in my house."

Startled by George's anger, Mom snapped her hand back from his.

"People will only be allowed in the salon and library," I said. "Declan painted reproductions so nobody will know you sold the originals. We've filled the house with furnishings. We'll explain that antiques and anything of value have been put into storage. People will understand."

"*You* don't understand." George's face reddened,

and he curled his fingers into the white blanket. "Losing that bloody house would be the best thing for me. It has made my life a living hell. It almost killed me, putting me in here. I plan to move south."

"South?" Fanny grasped my arm once again, thrown off balance by George's announcement. "To Brighton?"

George shook his head.

"Why, Brighton surely must have the most sunshine."

"Not as much as the Canary Islands." He glanced away, avoiding the distraught look on poor Fanny's face.

My heart sank. "Georgie Porgie" was sounding pretty good right about now.

"The Canary Islands?" Fanny's blue eyes widened, and her grip tightened on my arm. I bit down on my lower lip to keep from yelping out in pain.

George nodded. "I need more tolerable weather."

"When did you decide this?" Fanny muttered, her porcelain cheeks paling.

Afraid she was going to faint, I gestured to a chair for her to sit. She shook her head, determined to stay at George's bedside despite his devastating news.

"A while ago. My aunt Emily spends the winters there and found a suitable place for me. I need to make a down payment, so I had to put the estate up for sale sooner than I'd planned."

George was moving to the Canary Islands to be closer to a woman who hadn't even cared enough to respond to my e-mail about his life-threatening pneumonia? My breathing quickened.

"I see." Fanny wore a defeated expression. Not only had she known nothing of his decision, but she hadn't been involved in making it. "I could use a spot of tea."

George had to realize how Fanny felt about him. How could he not have respected her enough to have shared his plans? Had Diana made him that callous about love?

"I'll join you." Thomas wrapped an arm around Fanny's shoulder. "I won't be able to show my topiary if there's no event," he muttered as they walked out.

My chest tightened. I felt horrible that I'd given Thomas hope about showing his shrubs and that Fanny had been so optimistic about the future she'd practically moved into George's house. I couldn't believe the house wasn't part of George's identity. How could he just let it go after living there his entire life? How could he not have confided in Thomas and Fanny about his plans to move so far away? Thomas had been like the brother he'd never had, and Fanny was ten times better than the wife he *had* had.

"How can you just give up and let Enid win?" I asked. "I can't stand that woman after just a few days."

George peered down at the picture frame. "I'm not giving up. It's what I want. I'm sorry you went to all that trouble. You shouldn't have. Thomas and Fanny should have known better."

Rachel bit down on her lower lip, and the vein in her forehead pulsated. She was mentally counting to ten, trying not to lose it. She was as ticked off as I was with George.

Mom forced an uneasy smile. "This is George's decision to make, not ours. We'll support him with whatever he does."

Like hell we would! I didn't support the way he was

treating everyone. I opened my mouth to tell him that, and Declan grasped my elbow. "Tea sounds grand. Let's get some for everyone."

No way was tea fixing this nightmare. Yet I reined in my anger and allowed Declan to escort me from the room.

As soon as we were in the hallway, I said, "I can't believe George wants to lose the house and move to the Canary Islands. He's like a different man than he was in Prague."

"In all fairness to George, maybe it's his meds. Give him a few days to process the information you just threw at him."

"It's not the meds. He's adamant and appears to have had this planned for some time without anyone's knowledge. I thought we were helping him by organizing the event. It's one thing for him to be against it, but he doesn't have to be such an ass about it." I shook my head in disbelief. "My poor mom. This was her introduction to her brother? His rude behavior and anger-management issues? She must be devastated. The way he was treating poor Fanny and Thomas is inexcusable. He's showing more respect for some flippin' aunt he's never met. Where the hell is Emily Ryan right now? Soaking up the sun in the Canary Islands rather than coming to visit her dying nephew. I wish I'd never introduced them."

"It could be worse. He could be moving away to shack up with some woman who *isn't* related. That would kill Fanny."

"If he wants to live somewhere warmer, why not move to Florida to be closer to my mom and her sisters? It makes no sense."

"That's family. You take the good with the shite."

"What good? What good has finding George brought me? I've ruined Fanny's and Thomas's lives and upset my mom. Now she can be bitter toward her mother, brother, and me!"

What had I been thinking trying to find more family when I was just starting to get along with my immediate one?

No more ancestry research. I was done.

The past was better off left a mystery!

CHAPTER
SIXTEEN

Declan removed a painting from the salon wall—the woman seated at the desk, writing a letter in a sunny room. A shiver raced through me, the house's dampness once again chilling me to the bone. I rubbed my arms through Declan's blue sweater, glancing over at the ashes in the fireplace. I went over to make a fire to warm up the house before we picked up Mom from the hospital.

By the time Declan and I had returned from the cafeteria with tea, George had fallen asleep. Mom had insisted on being there when he woke up. She probably hadn't wanted to leave on such a sour note and was hoping George would wake up in a better mood. Fanny and Thomas hadn't spoken a word on the way home. When we dropped Fanny off at her impressive stone home, she said she'd be by later to pick up her belongings. Unless she was driving a U-Haul rather than her Aston Martin, Fanny wouldn't be picking up much. Her dream of moving in with George was crushed. Not only would Thomas be losing his home, but also the man who'd been like a brother to him. I'd lost the chance to save the estate and likely damaged my relationship with my only uncle.

Yet after the way he'd acted, I wasn't sure I cared.

Declan studied the painting. "This is my favorite."

"Take it. It's yours. They're all yours." I arranged kindling and wood in the fireplace.

I had no way to repay Declan for the money he'd spent on art supplies and advertising. I had over a thousand dollars in credit card debt from Facebook ads!

"I can't afford to keep taking stupid chances like this."

Declan's gaze darted to me. "You can't afford not to. And it wasn't stupid. Your sense of adventure is one reason I'm madly in love with you." A faint smile curled his lips. "It was grand painting again, even if nobody will see them."

He sounded as disappointed as Thomas had about not being able to show his shrubs to the public.

"I'm sorry." I clicked the fire-starter wand, and a flame materialized.

"Why? This was a good thing."

"I feel like everyone has been let down."

"I was all for doing this. Ya can't be blaming yourself. We all thought it was a brilliant idea."

I walked over to Declan and brushed a kiss against his lips. "Thank you for everything."

"Thanks to you, I'm painting again."

"You should take the paintings. Better than stashing them away in the shed for the new owners to toss. Or worse yet to sell and get the money for them."

The thought of the furnishings going back to the cold, damp shed, even the demented owl and flying monkey table, about made me burst into tears.

"I'm gonna go help Rachel in the kitchen, then go pack."

Declan and I were taking an early evening ferry back to Ireland. No reason to stay. Rachel and Mom would remain here until George came home. Next week they were coming to Ireland to visit Sadie and Seamus in the Midlands. Fingers crossed that introduction went much better.

Rachel was boxing up the teacups, hoping Nicole would buy them back even if we took a slight loss.

She set a cup on the counter next to a half dozen others. "Thought I would keep a few. Do you want some?"

I shrugged. George had offered me a cup and saucer from the Daly family china, and I wasn't even sure if I wanted that set.

"At least we might get our money back on the china. Refunding everyone's tickets might be a bit trickier."

My phone dinged, announcing the arrival of an e-mail. Nicholas Turney. My heart raced, then came to a screeching halt when I read his message. He hadn't found Grandma's baptismal record despite visiting every Catholic church within a twenty-mile radius of Killybog. My stomach dropped at the thought of returning to Milwaukee to live with my parents.

Even worse, at leaving Declan in Ireland. Along with Zoe, their parents, Sadie, Seamus, Nicholas Turney... What would happen with Declan and me if we lived four thousand miles apart and I was forbidden to return to Ireland for ninety days? He'd have to commute to Milwaukee!

"Shit," I muttered, dropping back against the counter.

"What's wrong?"

"Not only will I be leaving England, but I'll be leaving Ireland soon." It was time to fess up. "I can't find Grandma's birth or baptismal records. No documentation proving she was Irish or ever existed outside the US."

Rachel's gaze narrowed. "So you can't obtain dual citizenship?"

I shook my head.

"I'm assuming your boss doesn't know this? That I'm not the last to know?"

"I'm sorry. I know this will reflect poorly on you with Flanagan's."

"It reflects poorly on *you*, and not just with Flanagan's but with *me*. I can't believe you didn't tell me about this."

"I figured you'd be upset that I'd gone after the job, assuring Matthew McHugh I could get citizenship."

"I'm upset because we're sisters. And you're not the only one who has something vested in this. I want citizenship also."

My gaze narrowed. "You never mentioned that."

"Well, I've been thinking about it." She shook her head in frustration. "I could see one of her records not having been filed or lost, but both? You can't give up so easily."

"So easily? I've been searching over a month and recruiting everyone I know to help. Sadie found her mother's birth certificate at the registrar's office in

Mullingar. It didn't note her first name, Theresa. Maybe the same thing happened with Grandma's. But Nicholas verified parents' names on all the records during a three-year period around Grandma's birth year. What else am I supposed to do?"

"I don't know. I'm not the genealogist. You'll think of something. What about using her US naturalization papers or her Ellis Island record that shows her coming from Ireland and her birthplace was Killybog, where her sister Theresa Lynch lived?"

"The person I spoke with at immigration said those documents aren't sufficient."

"Well then, speak to someone else. Figure it out. We need to have dual citizenship." Rachel's breathing quickened. She looked like she needed citizenship as much as she was going to need an oxygen tank if she didn't calm down.

"Is this about Gerry?"

"No, it's not just about Gerry. It's about *me*."

So it was *partly* about Gerry.

"I wanted to be the estate's planner. To organize events and generate funds to keep this place going. Like booking art-mystery dinners for corporate events and holding garden parties to show off Thomas's flowers and shrubs. And..." She placed a hand to her forehead. "It doesn't matter. That plan is shot."

I scrambled to process Rachel's aspirations.

"So you'd have moved to Ireland to do that?"

She shrugged. "I'd have needed the flexibility of traveling back and forth without restrictions on the length of stay. I could have worked in Ireland and come here as needed."

Rachel had put some serious thought into this. She wasn't throwing it out there on a whim. Like I had when I'd decided to move to Ireland.

"I had no clue you were thinking about leaving Brecker."

"I'd have to stay there for a while. This wouldn't have been a full-time job at first. It would have been a volunteer position for the first year until I got the trust built up and could take a wage." Rachel's eyes watered, and she sucked in a shaky breath. "I have to reduce my stress."

"Is your kidney getting worse?"

Rachel shook her head. "I think"—she choked back a sob—"I'm losing my mind." A tear trailed down her cheek.

"Your mind is way sharper than mine. Look at how you were calculating math in your head when we were shopping for teacups. And..."

Rachel continued shaking her head. "That contract I forgot to confirm for Gemma's dinner wasn't my first mistake. I can't seem to remember anything lately." She swiped away several more tears.

I wrapped my sister in a hug, and she sobbed against my shoulder. "Your forgetfulness is the result of stress combined with the fact that maybe you're just over the job."

She drew back, wiping her eyes with her red sweater sleeve, smearing mascara on the fabric and under her eyes. "Maybe. Besides less stress, I'd have been making a difference, helping save the estate for George's sake and in Grandma's memory. And saving a historical home from becoming frickin' law offices. It would have given me a sense of purpose. Like your genealogy research gives you."

Great, one more person I'd given false hope.

"I'm done with genealogy research. I suck at it. I can't find Grandma's birth records or Gretchen's German grandpa. I might have just gotten my first breakthrough with Bernice and Gracie's Scottish rellies after a hundred hours of research. I found out all kinds of horrible stuff on Nigel's ancestor that I don't want to tell him, except I already spent his cash advance. And I hooked our uncle up with a rellie he's never even met, but he's leaving Fanny, Thomas, and the estate because of her."

"Genealogy research is like climbing Mount Everest."

"Yeah, something else I could never do."

"Seriously. Brecker once had a motivational speaker at a meeting who'd climbed Mount Everest. It takes ten days to reach basecamp at, like, seventeen thousand feet. But it takes forty days to go from basecamp to the summit, only another twelve thousand feet. Because you climb from base camp to camp one, spend the night, then go back to base camp. The next day you're back to camp one, spend a night, then camp two for a night, then back down to base camp. It's a series of ups and downs to make it to the summit. Your body has to slowly become acclimated with the lower oxygen levels."

"I wouldn't have the motivation or desire to climb a mountain."

"But you have perseverance, which you need for genealogy research."

"But I don't have a hundred hours in a day required to make progress tracing someone's line."

"The point is, a setback isn't a failure. It's often necessary before you can move forward. It's progress. Now you know where *not* to look for Grandma's records, so you are narrowing down where *to* look."

Kind of like *John* versus *Richard* McKinney...

"By the way, the speaker was feet from the summit when a snowstorm blew in. At that altitude, it took a minute to take one step, so she had to make the decision to go all the way back down Mount Everest. She did future climbs and eventually made it to the summit. You'll make it."

I was surprised that Rachel had faith in my abilities rather than offering to hire a qualified genealogist to locate the records. Whether it was online grocery shopping or a cleaning lady, she didn't hesitate to pay for convenience and competence. I wish she *would* hire a genealogist—I couldn't afford to!

"What if I never have another opportunity to do something that makes a difference?" she said. "That gives me a sense of purpose? I'm envious that you have a passion for genealogy. I'm good at my job but not passionate about it. Being driven to succeed and being passionate are two different things. And I'm envious you moved to Ireland. I'd have been too scared to make the move and give up my financial stability."

"I had no financial stability to give up."

"And I didn't know where I was going with Gerry. I still don't know, but I don't want a long-distance relationship that's doomed from the start." She paused, undoubtedly realizing she'd just said Declan and I were doomed. "But you made me realize it's time for a change. I can't get comfortable in a job I don't even like."

"Well, it wasn't such a bright move. My boss might fire me for letting him think my citizenship was in the bag. Getting a work permit sounds like a lot of red tape for him to go through when it's unlikely I'd get one. Besides, it's only valid for two years."

"Would give you time to work at getting citizenship. I mean, who knows how good of a researcher this Nicholas Turney is. He's old. Maybe his eyesight isn't so great at reading the chicken scratch on faded documents. This is too major to not double-check everything he did. You always say how inaccurate documents are. Part of that is human error."

"I haven't had time to drive out to the Midlands to do research."

"Now that you're no longer planning the mystery event, you'll have time."

Not really, when I was trying to learn a job I had no clue how to do. A job I might not have much longer.

❧ ❧

Rather than packing, I was sitting in George's rocking chair, handwriting him a heated letter, as Declan hadn't let me speak my piece at the hospital. No way was I returning to Ireland, leaving things unsaid. I scolded George for treating everyone so awful after we'd been worried sick about him and said he owed us an apology. My grip tightened on the pen. I feared it might snap in two and get ink all over me, but I couldn't relax the tension in my body. I told him that his behavior might be how the Dalys treated family, like his nasty cousin Enid, but this was not acceptable behavior for our family. That I might just be sorry I'd ever posted on that forum searching for my grandma's rellies. That I...

The doorbell echoed through the foyer and upstairs, followed by Mac's bark.

Crap. I was on a roll. However, Declan was hauling stuff back to the shed, and Rachel had run into Dalwick for a few bottles of wine. I took a deep breath, trying to get my labored breathing under control. I tossed my pen and paper on the chair and headed downstairs. I opened the door to find Fanny on the steps, her Aston Martin in the drive.

Mac gave her hand a lick, then trotted up the stairs.

She dabbed her red puffy eyes with a lace hanky. "I'm sorry to drop by unannounced, but I thought I would pick up some of my things, and I wanted to give you this. Pastor Alldridge dropped it off while I was out." She handed me an envelope.

George's baptismal record.

I ushered Fanny inside. "Would you like some tea?"

"No, thank you." A tear trailed down her cheek. "You wouldn't have some whiskey by chance, would you?"

"Of course."

I led Fanny into the library, where she burst into tears upon seeing her furniture. She collapsed on her blue velvet couch with the dramatic flair of Scarlett O'Hara, having been abandoned by Rhett Butler.

I grabbed the crystal decanter and poured Fanny a double. I joined her on the couch, handing her the drink. She downed half the liquor in one gulp.

I held up the envelope. "Have you looked at this?"

She shook her head.

I slipped the piece of paper from the envelope and unfolded it. The baptismal record noted George's birth parents as Bridget Coffey and Michael Daly.

"My grandma and Michael Daly were his parents."

Fanny smiled faintly and took another swig of whiskey.

I was unsure if I was relieved or disappointed. After today, did I want George to be my biological uncle, Mom's real brother? Not being related would have been an out. Or would it have? Even if we weren't related, could I have ditched George?

"I'll have my things moved out before George gets home. Please don't mention this to him. I'd be quite embarrassed if he found out how silly I've been."

"You weren't silly."

Yet I couldn't promise Fanny everything would be okay. I couldn't give her hope only to have it once again snatched away when love and happiness were within her grasp.

"I'm sorry about everything," I said.

Fanny looked baffled. "Why should you be sorry?"

I gestured at the furnished library. "All of this is my fault."

"Nonsense. It's better for me to stop pining for a man who doesn't reciprocate my feelings and to move on." She downed the rest of her drink.

Fanny's inspirational attitude reminded me of Rachel's Mount Everest pep talk. That even setbacks were progress and enabled you to move forward.

Fanny held out her glass. "Make it a triple."

It appeared I'd be playing a Bond girl, driving Fanny's Aston Martin, making sure they both made it home safely.

☙ ❧

Mac stood in the car's backseat, watching George's house fade into the distance. He whimpered, undoubtedly sensing we weren't merely heading into Dalwick to run errands or to Lancaster to visit George. I stared out the front window, unable to look back. Declan placed a hand on my leg, knowing I wasn't up to discussing our departure. Rachel had promised to drive Fanny home and to hire movers to help return her furnishings.

I stepped from the car to open the gate as Thomas walked up the gravel road from his cottage, carrying a potted shrub.

"Don't be too upset with George," he said. "He wasn't himself today."

I nodded faintly.

"Maybe you can return for a visit before he moves."

"I'll try."

"It's George's decision to not obtain closure. I'm glad I did, and it's thanks to you." He smiled. "I didn't realize how much my life would change when I sent you that e-mail merely a week ago."

Thomas felt his life had changed for the *better*?

"I contacted several newspapers and magazines today and arranged to show my topiary. I'd never have done such a thing before your arrival. You reminded me how good it feels to have others appreciate my work, my passion. You reminded me to follow my dreams."

I'd done all of that?

Thomas handed me the potted shrub. "It's a bonsai tree. A memento of your visit. May it bring you harmony and good fortune."

I smiled. "It already has."

I gave Thomas a hug good-bye.

CHAPTER SEVENTEEN

Mac had a much better return trip to Ireland. I was able to book him a kennel on the passenger deck so Declan and I could check on him during the ferry ride. However, it'd been my turn to feel sick to my stomach.

Sick over the thought of leaving Declan in Ireland.

We snagged a parking spot in front of Coffey's pub and decided to check on Gerry before schlepping everything upstairs. I texted Rachel to tell her I'd made it home safely and to see her reaction over me visiting Gerry. Moments later, she replied.

Picked up Mom. George was sleeping. I left your letter for him to read in the morning. Love ya.

I cringed at how angry my letter sounded. I didn't regret writing it, but maybe I shouldn't have given it to George. Maybe having merely written it was the therapy I'd needed to get over my hostility toward him. I debated asking Rachel to go to the hospital early tomorrow and destroy the letter before George read it...

No. I had every right to say the things I'd said. I should be more worried about Mom's reaction to the letter than George's. If he shared it with her, she wasn't going to be happy with me.

Declan opened the door to the pub.

Mac barked, pulling on the leash, wanting to keep walking.

I eyed him. "Why didn't you go when we got off the ferry?"

"He's grand. I'll take him."

I removed a plastic bag from my purse and handed it to Declan. "Thanks."

As they strolled off, my phone dinged. Rachel.

Tell Gerry hi.

I responded, *You tell him hi.*

Radio silence.

Coffey's pub was back to normal. The St. Patrick's Day decorations were gone, and mostly locals lined the bar. No slutty leprechaun flirting her heart out with Gerry, who didn't look his usual cheery self. He hadn't shaved in days and had dark circles under his eyes. I wanted to tell him that his conversation with Rachel had been the best thing for their relationship. It had been a wake-up call for her.

Gerry glanced over and gave me a faint smile.

"How ya doing?" I slipped onto a barstool.

He shrugged. "Maybe honesty isn't always the best policy."

Today was my day for being open and honest with everyone, so I admitted my complications with obtaining citizenship and Rachel's desire to also have it and to be the estate's event planner.

"I'm sure you're a big part of her reason for wanting citizenship. Yet it's not looking promising. My historian friend came up empty."

"I know a bloke who could come up with your granny's birth record for a few quid."

I arched a brow. "The original?"

"Best not be asking questions." He winked.

I believed he'd go to those great lengths so Rachel could live in Ireland.

Would *I* go to such lengths to remain in Ireland?

"She and Mom are staying in England until George gets home and back on his feet. They'll be here next weekend to visit our rellies. She'll have to be back to work after that, but my mom might stay longer. My dad might have to grocery shop for the first time in his life."

Gerry's phone rang. He grabbed it off the back bar by the register. He peered over at me, smiling. "Rachel."

A sense of relief washed over me. At least something might have turned out right today.

☘ ☘

Declan, Mac, and I entered my apartment, and I dropped my carry-on bag on the floor. I flipped on the light and stared in confusion at my bed, no longer deflated on the floor. It was a foot *off* the floor—a queen-size mattress with a yellow duvet and a white headboard that matched a dresser.

Mac ran over and sprang up onto the bed. He circled around before lying down and curling up in a ball.

"Didn't want ya to be going broke buying inflatable beds."

"You bought all this?"

Was this why Declan hadn't had any luck apartment hunting? Because he hadn't even been looking? He planned on moving in?

Mom had been right?

"Would have bought the matching lockers but didn't figure one would fit on each side of the bed."

I tried to remain calm. "You shouldn't have done this after spending all that money on an event that isn't even going to happen."

"You don't like it?"

"No, of course, I like it. And I'll pay you back."

How, I had no clue. I'd be paying off that friggin' Facebook ad for months.

"It's a gift. You're not paying me back."

"Yes, I am."

"Then consider it Mac's bed, or my furniture I'm keeping here so I have somewhere to sleep...with you." He brushed a kiss against my lips. When I didn't respond, he drew back. "Right, then, not exactly the romantic evening I had planned. No worries. I respect you not wanting to live together straight away."

"Doesn't look like it," I muttered.

He ran a frustrated hand through his hair.

I shook my head. "I'm sorry. It's just..."

"You think I'm trying to control ya with money and gifts?" Declan's gaze sharpened. "That I'm being like Andy? There's a difference between being dependent on a man and allowing someone who loves you to help out." He snagged Mac's leash off the hook by the door.

"Come on, Mac. Time for a walk."

The dog's ears perked up at the word *walk*. He hopped off the bed and followed Declan out the door.

I stared at the closed door. Was I an ungrateful bitch or what? My stomach tossed at the thought of Declan comparing himself in any way to Andy. He was absolutely nothing like that...

Omigod. I'd forgotten all about Andy having called Mom.

His call hadn't been weighing heavy on me, affecting me physically and emotionally. An empowering feeling rose inside me. A more powerful feeling than when I wore my *Póg Mo Thóin* undies. I suddenly felt in control of my relationship with Andy. That *he* no longer controlled *me*. It wasn't to say I was fully recovered and at times self-doubt wouldn't still be lurking at the back of my mind, thanks to that bastard. However, I had to continue moving forward. No way was I moving back to Milwaukee.

I had to keep climbing Mount Everest!

I filled the teakettle with water, needing some serious caffeine if I was going to stay up all night searching for Grandma's record. If I couldn't find it, then I had to figure out a way to get a work visa. Or maybe I'd quit work and enroll at Trinity College. It sounded like a student visa was easier to get than a work one. Forget the fact that I'd just started paying on my student loan this month.

The door slowly opened. Mac trotted inside and hopped up onto the couch. Declan walked in carrying the leash, not having made it outside. He peered cautiously over at me.

"I'm sorry," he said. "I'll return the furniture. I just want you to be able to do your genealogy research without worrying about bills. I'm financially in a place to help you. I wasn't with Shauna, and I regret not supporting her when she wanted to quit her job and pursue her passion. She loved painting more than anything, more than I did."

Eyes watering, I walked over and hugged Declan. "I'm sorry. I'm just stressed out about everything right now." I drew back. "The only good thing that has happened today is I remembered Andy called."

Declan's gaze narrowed. "That's a good thing, is it? When was this?"

"He called my parents' house for me. My mom told me when she got to England. I honestly had so much else going on I forgot all about it."

His lips curled into a smile. "That's brilliant ya forgot."

I nodded. "It is."

"Gonna ring him back, are ya?"

"No. I don't give a crap what he has to say."

The teakettle whistled.

I went over and grabbed two of Grandma's cups from the shelf. "That would have been so cool if I'd found a Flannery's teacup at Nicole's shop. I don't plan on researching my Flannery line for a while—I have all the family I can handle for now. But it still would have been cool."

"Knowing their factory was near Arklow is a great start. Your great-granny was likely born in the area."

What if *Grandma* had been born in Arklow?

My gaze darted to Declan. "What if my grandma's mother, Mary, had gone home to give birth because she'd been having complications? Or she'd been visiting her parents and my grandma came earlier than expected? Just because my grandma's siblings were born in Killybog doesn't mean she was for sure." Nicholas and I had both done a countrywide search of civil indexes, but nothing had jumped out at us. However, I hadn't spent much time searching outside of County Westmeath.

Why hadn't I thought of this before?

Declan and I booted up our laptops and frantically typed away, searching genealogy sites and indexes. After an hour of trying various spellings and birth years, I came across a possibility. "Here's a Bridget *Clauffey* born in Arklow, January to March 1916. What if the name is supposed to be *Coffey*?"

"Not familiar with Clauffey. Once knew a Claffey."

"It's just an index. Doesn't list parents' names." I searched for other Clauffeys born in Arklow the years surrounding Grandma's birth year. "Not one other Clauffey was born anywhere near that date in Arklow." A sense of excitement zipped through me. "What if this is it? I need to get a copy."

"Let's find the registrar's office in County Wicklow." Declan typed away on his laptop. "Bray. Just south of Dublin."

"If the original certificate has the wrong surname and doesn't note Mary's maiden name, maybe my grandma's baptismal record would have the correct names. The Catholic parish records are only online for Wicklow until 1900. We'll have to go to the church in Arklow to search the originals."

"I'll go to Bray tomorrow and if necessary make a trip down to Arklow," Declan said.

My heart raced. I wanted to call in sick so I could go with Declan and be there when he found Grandma's records. So we could celebrate together.

I smiled. "Let's celebrate."

"Grand idea. Fancy a pint with Gerry?"

"I'm sure he's drinking to Rachel's call right now, but I'd rather celebrate alone." I gave him a flirty smile, grasping hold of his hand. We walked past Mac snoring on the couch and over to *our* new bed.

CHAPTER
EIGHTEEN

The following morning I wanted to hop off the bus on the way to work and Uber it back home to go with Declan to County Wicklow. He'd be waiting at the door when the registrar's office opened. I tried not to be overly hopeful in case it wasn't Grandma's birth record, but my gut told me it was. I couldn't let a little thing like a name documented or transcribed incorrectly dampen my spirits. Or the fact that Grandma hadn't lived in County Wicklow.

Besides historical records often being incorrect, what about family lore? How often was that wrong? Nigel's family believed their ancestor was of royalty when he'd actually been shipped off to prison. What if Gretchen's grandpa wasn't from Germany? He could have lived in Germany but not been *born* there. I needed to search birth records for the surrounding countries.

I had a passion for ancestry research. I merely lacked experience. Yet Nicholas Turney had way more experience than me and hadn't considered the fact that Grandma could have been born in Arklow. Or maybe he'd searched the Arklow records but Clauffey hadn't jumped out at him as a possibility. Like Rachel said, it'd taken years for her to become a skilled meeting planner, a job she wasn't passionate about. Maybe it wouldn't take me quite as long to become skilled at a job I *was* passionate about.

I took the plunge and e-mailed Nigel, tactfully dropping the bomb about his convict great-grandpa, whose ethnicity was still a mystery. He could decide whether or not to tell his mom. I owed him the truth.

My phone rang. Mom.

Had George shared my letter with her and she was calling to yell at me? I debated answering the call, not wanting to let any negative energy zap my positive attitude.

I took a deep breath, then answered with a perky hello.

Mom was sobbing on the other end.

"What's wrong? Is George okay?"

She inhaled a shaky breath. "Yeah, I guess so."

She *guessed* so?

"Then why are you crying?" Was she disappointed in me over the letter? Had I made my mom cry? My chest tightened.

"He's better physically, being released tomorrow, but I'd hoped he'd be better emotionally by this morning. He's...just not who I thought he'd be."

Anger growled at the back of my throat, and I tightened my grasp on the phone.

"Where's Rachel?"

Mom sniffled. "Getting us tea. I'm in the restroom."

That reminded me of my previous job, having to hide out in hotel bathrooms for a moment of peace to regain my sanity.

"You and Rachel should do something fun today. How about going to that cute little café in Dalwick? Sit on a bench by the river and read a book. Do something relaxing."

She blew her nose. "That might be a good idea."

"Tell George you'll see him later. You don't owe him an explanation."

We didn't owe George a damn thing!

My entire body trembled with anger. As if I hadn't felt bad enough over George's scene at the hospital yesterday. Rather than hopping an Uber back home to join Declan to County Wicklow, I wanted to hop a ferry to England and give George a piece of my mind.

"Thanks, dear. I feel better. Sorry to call when you're probably on your way to work. Didn't mean to get your day off to a bad start."

I wanted to tell her that this would hopefully turn out to be my best day in a long time. Yet I didn't want to give her even a glimmer of hope in the off chance it ended up not being Grandma's birth record.

I'd given her way too much hope about her half brother, and look how that had turned out.

I arrived at work a half hour early, determined to put the bounce back in my step after Mom's phone call. In less than two hours, Declan would have Grandma's birth record in hand. Rather than reading through the proposal I'd received from a Florence hotel, I found myself on Scotland's record site, searching for a James McKinney born to a *Richard* and Mary.

"How's the incentive planning going?" Gemma said behind me.

Startled, I lowered my laptop screen. Crap. I spun around in my chair to find her red lips curled into a smirk.

"Great. Should have estimated budgets done by the end of the day, tomorrow at the latest."

Her *cheeky* smile faded. "Mr. McHugh would like to see you in an hour." She strutted off in her green dress and heels.

Not even Gemma was going to burst my bubble today.

My boss undoubtedly wanted an update on the incentive trip and to verify that I hadn't been on vacay in England. I three-hole-punched the contracts I'd printed and added some additional paperwork to fill up a medium-size binder, proving I'd been hard at work.

An hour later, I was seated in front of the CEO.

"We're having to change the incentive dates to September," he said. "Sorry about that after all the information you've collected."

Ugh. So I'd have to contact twenty-two hotels to verify availability and rates for the new dates?

My phone dinged. It had to be Declan. Few people

texted me. My heart raced, and my fingers itched to reach down and slip the phone from my purse.

"I know you wanted to plan the Kerry meeting, but I feel you should hand it off to Gemma. She's at a bit of a lull at the moment. I think it's best to have the meetings evenly distributed. I'm afraid I may have overestimated our need for a full-time planner." His phone rang, and he excused himself to answer it.

Was he going to fire me?

Rather than panic racing through me, excitement flittered around my chest like a hummingbird on steroids. I wouldn't actually get fired but rather let go due to an insufficient workload. I needed to create cards for my genealogy business and have Gerry distribute them to fellow pub owners. And Nicholas Turney mentioned a local B and B referred people to him for ancestry research assistance. I could reach out to B and Bs. I needed to build a website...

The CEO finished his call. "So for now the position will be more part time. Eventually it will grow into full time, and then we can hire you as a Flanagan employee."

Eventually I wouldn't be there.

"I hope this doesn't put you in a financial bind."

It did, but it also put me in an incredibly elated mood.

"Talk to Rachel. Brecker likely has some meetings to supplement your workload. After this month, we'll probably need to contract by the meeting rather than by the month."

Brecker's CEO had decided to contract me monthly because we didn't know when my citizenship would come through, making me eligible for full-time employment with Flanagan's.

I nodded, slowly standing. "Sure. I'll do that."

I'd been fighting Gemma to keep a job I really didn't want. This job was a means to an end. To get me off the road and provide a more stable work environment with a steady paycheck. Most of all, to get me to Ireland and closer to Declan. Even part time, Flanagan's would provide some stable income.

I had to keep this job until my debt was paid down and I could transition into a full-time genealogy business. It would take time to build up clientele and my research skills. Rachel would undoubtedly be quitting her job in the near future. She wouldn't have reason to care if I later quit.

As I walked out the door, I slipped my phone from my purse. Declan had texted a photo of Grandma's notarized birth record, which had her mother's name correctly documented as Mary Flannery but father as Patrick *Clauffey*. I let out a frustrated groan. Declan had left messages for the Catholic priests in the Arklow area, asking if he could access their churches' baptismal records today.

Stay positive.

I stopped at Gemma's desk as she hung up the phone. "I guess you're going to be planning the Kerry meeting now."

She arched a brow. "Messed it up, did ya?"

"No, I'm just pretty busy."

"I guess I can take it on if you feel you can't do it." She flashed me a victorious grin that I'd normally want to wipe off her smug face.

Let Gemma believe she'd won. When, really, I knew I had.

✣✣ ✣✣

I was sitting at my desk, eating a salad from the cafeteria, when Declan texted, attaching a pic of Grandma's baptismal record. Parents were noted as Mary Flannery and Patrick *Coffey*. The sponsors were Catherine and James Flannery.

I let out a delighted squeal, causing several curious coworkers to pop up from behind their cubicle walls.

I confirmed I'd be home at four to pop my application in the mail. I started typing a letter to include with my packet, pleading my case. I asked if my paperwork could be expedited for an additional fee or if they would allow me to extend my ninety-day tourist visa due to the delay in locating my grandma's records.

I forwarded Grandma's docs to Rachel, along with the website link for the citizenship application. Declan had purchased three notarized copies of Grandma's birth certificate in case Mom also decided to pursue Irish citizenship. After our earlier conversation, I highly doubted it. She might not even return to Ireland to visit me. She couldn't wait to get the hell out of Dodge. I couldn't wait to get to *England*.

If George thought my letter sounded angry, just wait until he *heard* what I had to say!

CHAPTER NINETEEN

The following morning, Declan, Mac, and I took the 8:00 a.m. ferry to Wales. We arrived at the hospital just before noon to help Mom and Rachel take George home. I thought it best that George ride with them rather than Declan and me. I needed time to calm my nerves and mentally prepare for my conversation with him. Not that driving down George's narrow sheep-filled road was the best stress reducer, but at least I wasn't behind the wheel. I stared out at a field of sheep, my shoulders relaxing. I loved the animals when I wasn't chasing them away from Thomas's shrubs.

Rachel pulled up to the gate, and we stopped behind her. I hopped out and unlocked it. After Rachel and Declan drove in, I secured the entrance. We drove up to the house and parked. Declan grabbed George's suitcase from the trunk. We all walked toward the house in eerie silence as if we were about to enter a church for George's funeral rather than his home. This was the day we'd all been waiting for since we'd arrived here a week ago. Thanks to George, it wasn't the joyous occasion it should have been.

We stepped inside to a warm, cozy salon. Heat emanated from the iron registers, and flames flickered in the fireplace.

George peered down at his shoes rather than taking in the newly furnished surroundings. "Feels awfully hot in here." His harsh and judgmental tone, implying we'd run up the fuel bill, made my entire body tense.

Mom managed a tight smile. "We thought it best that you come home to a heated house after your pneumonia."

Rachel glared at our uncle. "We had to replace the boiler. Paid for it with some of the books in the shed."

George's top lip curled into a sneer. "Hope you didn't sell the *Mary Poppins* book."

We all exchanged cautious glances, silently agreeing not to admit we had sold the classic. How about a thank-you for taking care of the broken boiler and creatively financing it? I clamped my teeth down on my lower lip so hard I about squealed out in pain.

George eyed the flying monkey table. "Always hated that table."

"Right, then." Declan peered over at Rachel, who looked like she was one snide comment away from blowing up, and at Mom, who was about to burst into tears. "Fancy some tea and scones?"

Declan gave my hand a good-luck squeeze before he fled after Rachel and Mom already halfway to the kitchen.

George slid a discreet glance over at the artwork hanging on the wall. All the paintings remained except for the one of the woman ' writing the letter, which Declan had taken. George's gaze swept the room. His breathing quickened, a faint whistling sound escaping from between his thin lips.

"Maybe you should sit down." I gestured to Fanny's blue velvet wingback chair in the corner.

"I'm fine," he snapped.

"I don't think you're *fine*."

He looked surprised by my sarcastic tone yet continued avoiding my gaze. The fact that he didn't even have the courtesy to look at me fueled my anger, but I continued with a calm and matter-of-fact tone.

"And I'm not just talking about you needing to sit rather than stand. I'm talking about *this you* not being fine compared to the *you* I met in Prague. This cranky, unappreciative, rude *you* versus the kind, caring, and considerate *you* I first met. The *you* who should be thanking us for helping you out rather than—"

George held up a halting hand. "I get your point." He gazed over at the paintings with a glassy-eyed haze and muttered, "Yes indeed, I get your point." Nodding, he slowly walked over and collapsed down on Fanny's blue velvet chair. His cheeks grew pale.

My heart raced. Was he having a stroke or a heart attack?

He bent over and covered his face with his hands, sobbing uncontrollably. His rapid transition from angry to distraught threw me for a loop. I went over and knelt down by him, placing a hand on his back.

"Omigod, George. What is it? Why are you acting so different? I want to believe that was the real you I'd met in Prague. Please tell me what this is about."

After some more crying, George lowered his hands from his face, his eyes bloodshot, his complexion red and blotchy. He pulled a cotton hanky from the pocket of his tan slacks. "I owe everyone an apology for my abhorrent behavior. I've been most rude and unappreciative and every other bad thing you said." He glanced around. "Especially after all everyone has done for me."

A tear trailed down his cheek, and he slipped my unopened letter from his jacket pocket. "Couldn't bring myself to read it. Was afraid you'd put me in my place, as you should have. However, I couldn't bear to face the disappointment your family must have in me right now."

"If we'd known the event was going to upset you so much, we never would have planned it. Thomas seriously believed it would give you closure. It'd made him feel better."

"Thomas has always been like a brother to me. I cannot believe how I treated him. I am overwhelmed at what lengths everyone went to assist me, and I owe you an explanation." He took a deep breath and eased it out. "My first thought when you mentioned the event was that the cold case would be solved and the truth would be known. I panicked, and pushing everyone away seemed like the best thing to do."

The truth?

"Well, the truth is, there is no case to solve. I know who stole the artwork. I've known for eight years. Suppose I always suspected it but couldn't bring myself to confirm it. I didn't know until Diana left that...she'd orchestrated the entire theft. When I asked her to please stay, she confessed. Guess she felt I would let her leave once I learned the truth."

I slipped my hand around George's and gave it a comforting squeeze, my eyes watering. "Oh, George, I'm so sorry."

"I was a fool to ever marry her, and she played me for the fool I was. I was ashamed and didn't want anyone to know, especially not Fanny. She deserves much better than a foolish old man."

"You're not foolish. Diana's damsel-in-distress act over the theft was good enough to convince Thomas she was innocent. Besides, love isn't based on reasoning." I smiled. "And Fanny loves you."

"I'm sure her feelings have recently changed. I'll never forgive myself for the way I spoke to her and made her feel so unimportant when I can't imagine a day in my life without her."

"She still cares a lot for you."

A hopeful smile curled his thin lips. "I'd lost my will to fight after Diana left. I gave up on everything, on life. I don't want to see the estate go to that bloody solicitor's firm or for Enid to profit one penny from the sale. I don't wish to move down the road let alone to the Canary Islands. Another lie. Emily had suggested the Canary Islands would be good for my health, but I hadn't seriously considered moving there. Once again, I panicked and feared I'd need to run away so nobody learned the truth."

George let out a heavy sigh. "Even if we held this mystery event, it might help immediate bills, but what about long term? An estate is in constant need of funds.

It's very taxing not only on my physical well-being but also my emotional."

I gave his hand another comforting squeeze before releasing it and standing. "I know someone with ideas for maintaining the estate."

He dropped back against the chair, looking relieved yet drained by his confession.

"Would you like me to explain everything to the others?"

He nodded. "If you wouldn't mind. I fear I am not up to retelling such a sad tale."

"I'll be right back."

I flew from the room and into the kitchen where everyone sat around the table, drinking red wine rather than tea. Even Mom was drinking. One of George's expensive bottles of wine sat empty on the table.

I quickly recounted George's confession.

Tears trailed down Mom's cheeks. Rachel let out a relieved sigh, then downed the rest of her wine.

Declan gave me a hug and kissed me right in front of Mom. "I knew you'd be grand."

I smiled anxiously at my sister. "George would like to give the art-mystery event a go but has some concerns about financing the estate long term. Thought you might want to share your ideas."

Rachel shot up from the chair, looking determined and inspired. She marched out of the kitchen, leaving behind the workaholic, stressed-out Rachel and her bad kidney.

CHAPTER TWENTY

One Week Later

"Seriously, darling"—Zoe placed a long white-gloved hand on a gentleman's arm—"you must come to London next week to see my film's premiere. It's simply the bee's knees. All the critics are raving about it."

A dozen guests surrounded Zoe in the salon, snapping selfies with her as if she were a true celebrity. She pulled off the blue chiffon dress quite well, and her fake emerald necklace sparkled under the fully lit chandelier. She struck a pose as the professional photographer we'd hired snapped a shot.

"Guinness, come here, my pet."

Rachel had changed Mac's name to fit her role of a wealthy beer heiress. She gave Mac's gold leash a slight tug as he attempted to take off up the stairs. He wasn't happy about the leash or the faux diamond-studded collar. However, he had to remain on a leash in case he freaked out over the flying monkey table and scared the guests.

"Champagne, luv?" Gerry Coffey snagged two flutes of sparkling cider off the tray of a passing waitress dressed in a black uniform, played by Nicole Duvall. "Thank you, madame."

"My pleasure, sir." Nicole had the British accent down to a tee. Being an actress, she might have mastered it while still living in the States.

Several actors were assisting today and would be taking over our roles for future events as we couldn't all be there during the week, except for George and Fanny.

"It matches your dress brilliantly," Gerry said.

"As your suit so nicely matches my family's stout."

Gerry, her gentleman friend, was decked out in a vintage dark-brown suit with a cream-colored oxford and bow tie. He gave her a kiss, and their lips lingered. Thankfully, their lovey-dovey behavior wasn't an act. Rachel wasn't yet sure where their relationship was headed, but she wanted to find out.

George looked dapper in his black tux and bow tie. He'd feared he'd have to have it altered after losing weight in the hospital, but Fanny's scones with clotted cream had helped him put on a few pounds. Probably not the diet the doctor had recommended.

George gestured to the blue wingback chair in the corner. "I do believe blue suits the home quite nicely." He patted Fanny's hand, her arm looped through his. "As do you, my dear."

Fanny's porcelain cheeks flushed pink. She had on the blue dress and white fur stole she'd worn in her boudoir photo. The two were perfect for the role of an eccentric millionaire couple, the estate's owners. I doubted it would be long before they weren't acting and Fanny and her blue furnishings would be right at home.

"I'm so glad I have my friends and family by my side today. It's made opening the house much less difficult than I'd imagined and a bit of fun."

"We wouldn't want to be anywhere else," Mom said.

We raised our sparkling ciders and toasted to George living a long and prosperous life on the Daly Estate. The only person currently not present was Thomas, who was giving several newspaper and magazine reporters a guided tour of his topiary and garden. Rachel had sent the press free tickets to cover the event.

George smiled at the painting of the woman seated at a desk and writing a letter, which Declan had returned for the occasion. "It was always my favorite. I missed it most of all. Feels good to have it back home where it belongs."

"It is quite lovely," a woman said. "But would you be willing to part with it for say...five?"

Everyone's gazes darted to Declan.

He nodded. "Sounds grand. I can have another one painted by the week's end."

"Lovely," she said. "And we'll have five thousand cash for you then." She and her husband strolled off, continuing to browse the artwork.

Declan let out a low whistle, fanning himself with the red ascot tied loosely around the collar of his white oxford. "Jaysus. Would be taking me two weeks of traveling to make that much quid."

He wouldn't even have to travel around *Ireland* now that he could pursue his passion and natural talent as a career.

George patted Declan on the back. "Well, young man, I do believe you have a new lucrative career painting stolen artwork."

Declan smiled. "It may prove quite profitable for us both."

"I have plenty of empty rooms on the upper floor that would do quite nicely as an artist studio when you visit on the weekends, as I hope you two will."

Declan and I nodded. We planned on spending many weekends at the estate, visiting George and assisting Rachel. She'd already booked a corporate art-mystery event and an intimate wedding for an art dealer. With all of Rachel's planning-industry connections worldwide, she'd have no difficulty booking special events at the estate.

"Too bad the painting is going to get swiped again." I brushed a nervous hand down the front of my jade-colored dress, mentally rehearsing my role as Detective Shaw of Scotland Yard. As soon as Fanny screamed out that the painting was missing...

Declan clasped hold of my hand. "Stop fidgeting. You'll be grand." He placed a kiss to the top of my hand, and my shoulders relaxed.

Fanny's gaze narrowed on an elderly gentleman in a dark suit entering the front door with a woman in a long black dress. "What is *he* doing here?"

"Who is it?" Rachel asked.

"Martin Edwards, a partner at Edwards and Price," George said. "Enid's lawyer."

Rachel and I marched over to the man, everyone following.

"Didn't you hear," I said. "The house is no longer on the market. And Enid has no claim to any of the furnishings."

The man looked baffled. "I beg your pardon?"

"Did you really think George would sell you the place when you're representing Enid?" Rachel asked.

"I do apologize, but I haven't a clue what you are referring to. Enid Daly? I can't recall the last time we've spoken. She's left several messages. I just returned from our holiday home in Scotland."

"Then why did she have a letter on your company stationary detailing her lawsuit against George?" I asked.

He arched an intrigued brow. "That's quite interesting indeed. I must be asking her the same thing." He strolled off with his wife to admire the artwork.

"That bitch was lying the entire time?" Rachel said. "Did she think we wouldn't find out?"

"She probably figured we'd make a deal while George was in the hospital and she'd flee the country before we figured it out," Mom said.

Right on cue, Enid marched through the front door in her typical riding attire. Why bother to dress appropriately for an event she hadn't bought a ticket to attend anyway? She stalked across the salon toward us.

"Here to pick up your assistant?" Rachel gestured to the flying monkey table.

Enid glared at Rachel, then directed her attention to George. "I wouldn't be here if you had the courtesy to return my phone calls. I am more than willing to settle this whole thing amicably and out of court if you would at least have the respect to discuss the matter."

"Advised your lawyer, have ya?" Declan said. "That you prefer to resolve the lawsuit out of court?"

Our gazes darted over to the lawyer and his wife enjoying Zoe's theatrics. Enid followed our gazes. Her eyes widened, and she went pale. She turned on her bootheels and made a swift getaway. Hopefully, to never be seen again.

"Slag," Fanny and I both said.

"Well, that couldn't have worked any better if we'd planned it," Mom said.

While a couple complimented George on his home and the event, Mom went into the library to do a head count.

She returned. "We're still missing two people. I'll have the servers start inviting guests into the library for tea."

We all clinked champagne glasses. "Let the show begin."

Mom, Rachel, and Gerry headed into the library, while Declan, George, Fanny, and I hung back.

Thomas, dressed in the brown tweed suit and green wellies, walked in the front door with the last two guests and the media. He gave us the thumbs-up and smiled proudly for Rachel's photographer snapping their pic. He led them into the library to join the others.

A man dressed in jeans and a casual tan jacket entered the front door. "Sorry. I don't have a ticket. I saw the flyer in town for your event. I'm passing through on my way to Glasgow to visit my son at the university. My name's Robert Daly. Thought it would be nice to get a snap of myself in front of the Daly Estate. You never know. There might be a family connection."

"Caity here would be able to help you determine if there is one," George said. "I only know as far back as my grandfather who bought the estate in 1860."

I nodded. "Sure. I'd be happy to help."

The guy seemed more intrigued by the flying monkey table and the other eclectic décor than tracing his Daly family tree.

Outside of the Coffey couple in Scotland, I'd solved all my genealogy mysteries. Nigel decided his ancestor's true identity would remain our little secret. Now that I knew James McKinney's father was Richard—not John—I'd found the children's birth records in Glasgow. I'd started tracing the family forward and hoped to have found descendants before Bernice and Gracie's upcoming Scotland trip. I'd located Gretchen's grandfather's birth record in Hungary rather than Germany. They'd moved to Munich when he was a boy. This discovery would enable her to obtain citizenship through her Hungarian grandfather, whereas Germany only allowed citizenship through parents. Hungary was part of the EU, allowing Gretchen to buy her mountain cottage in Bavaria. It had been my shining hour.

Declan leaned in. "Not sure how interested this bloke is in his family tree, but how about a Daly clan gathering here? You'd get loads of clients."

I smiled. "Excellent idea."

Robert Daly peered up the stairs. "This is one of the most magnificent staircases. It would be perfect... Would you mind if I take a snap of it?"

"By all means," George said.

He took a pic with his cell phone. "I can't believe I've never been here. I thought I'd visited all the country homes in this area."

"It's a private estate, just recently opened to the public," George said.

The man nodded, slipping a card from his wallet and handing it to George. "I'm the location scout for *Sunnyvale Street.*"

Fanny gasped. "Oh my. How lovely to meet you."

That was the horrific soap opera I refused to admit I'd been sucked in to watching at the hospital.

"Is that a nighttime show?" George's overly innocent tone seemed rather suspicious. Was he a *Sunnyvale Street* closet watcher?

"I can't believe you've never seen it," Fanny said. "That is one of the most magnificent shows on television."

"Is it now?" George said.

"I'm thinking this would make a great location for one of next season's story lines. It would merely be a few episodes."

Omigod, what incredible exposure for the estate!

"I can't say who, but a certain couple will be getting married."

Fanny gasped. "They aren't?"

George and I shared a mental eye roll.

Was that woman nuts marrying that cheating bastard? I wondered if it took five years to get a divorce in England like it did in Ireland, because that marriage was doomed.

"I'll go get my sister, Rachel. She organizes the estate's special events."

"I'm late to meet my son. Please give her my card and ask her to get in touch next week." He snapped a few more pics on his way out.

Declan's phone dinged, and he slipped it from his suit jacket pocket. He read the text and glanced over at me. "It's from a Susan Flannery. I gave my number to the priest who found your granny's baptismal certificate. Asked him to forward to any possible Flannery relations in his parish. This Susan says she's a rellie and wants your e-mail address."

I smiled. "Wow, too bad all my genealogy research wasn't that easy." No matter what happened with my Flannery family, I had to remember what Declan said: *You take the good with the shite.*

Remembering a call had come through earlier, I slipped my phone from the small black beaded purse on my shoulder. I listened to a voicemail message from Emily Ryan calling from the Canary Islands, inquiring on George's health. She hadn't checked up on him because she'd also been ill for the past few weeks with a flu. She wanted to let me know that my application for Irish citizenship was being expedited, so no need for me to leave the country when my ninety-day visa expired.

I took back every nasty thought I'd had about Emily being a neglectful aunt. But how had she known...

I glanced over at George. "Seems Emily Ryan has a connection to someone with Irish immigration services and my citizenship is being expedited." The one person I hadn't asked for assistance.

George smiled. "It's good to have connections."

I returned his smile, grasping hold of his hand and giving it a squeeze. "It's good to have *family*."

Declan brushed a kiss to my lips. "Yes, it is."

Who knew how large my family tree would end up by the time it stopped growing, if it ever did.

Hopefully, it didn't.

COMING FEBRUARY 2020

When in
Doubt Don't
Chicken Out

The Travel Mishaps of Caity Shaw

USA Today Bestselling Author
Eliza Watson

AUTHOR'S NOTE

Thank you so much for reading *Live to Fly Another Day*. If you enjoyed Caity's adventures, I would greatly appreciate you taking the time to leave a review. Reviews encourage potential readers to give my stories a try, and I would love to hear your thoughts. My monthly newsletter features genealogy research advice, my latest news, and frequent giveaways. You can subscribe at www.elizawatson.com.

ABOUT ELIZA WATSON

When Eliza isn't traveling for her job as an event planner, or tracing her ancestry roots through Ireland, she is at home in Wisconsin working on her next novel. She enjoys bouncing ideas off her husband, Mark, and her cats Frankie and Sammy.

Connect with Eliza Online

www.elizawatson.com

www.facebook.com/ElizaWatsonAuthor

www.instagram.com/elizawatsonauthor

Printed in the USA
CPSIA information can be obtained
at www.ICGtesting.com
LVHW011832011223
765460LV00011B/360